ROCKVILLE PUBLIC LIBRARY

3 4035 15420 3315

P9-DMF-801

THE CHARMING LIFE OF IZZY MALONE

ALSO BY JENNY LUNDQUIST

The Wondrous World of Violet Barnaby

Seeing Cinderella

Plastic Polly

The Princess in the Opal Mask

The Opal Crown

THE CHARMING LIFE OF IZZY MALONE

JENNY LUNDQUIST

CHILDREN'S DEPARTMENT
Rockville Public Library
Vernon, CT 06066

Aladdin

New York London Toronto Sydney New Delhi

If you purchased this book without a cover, you should be aware that this book is stolen property. It was reported as "unsold and destroyed" to the publisher, and neither the author nor the publisher has received any payment for this "stripped book."

This book is a work of fiction. Any references to historical events, real people, or real places are used fictitiously. Other names, characters, places, and events are products of the author's imagination, and any resemblance to actual events or places or persons, living or dead, is entirely coincidental.

ALADDIN

An imprint of Simon & Schuster Children's Publishing Division

1230 Avenue of the Americas, New York, New York 10020

First Aladdin paperback edition September 2017

Text copyright © 2016 by Jenny Lundquist

Cover illustration copyright © 2016 by Ilaria Falorsi

Also available in an Aladdin hardcover edition.

All rights reserved, including the right of reproduction in whole or in part in any form.

ALADDIN and related logo are registered trademarks of Simon & Schuster, Inc.

For information about special discounts for bulk purchases, please contact Simon & Schuster Special Sales at 1-866-506-1949 or business@simonandschuster.com.

The Simon & Schuster Speakers Bureau can bring authors to your live event. For more information or to book an event contact the Simon & Schuster Speakers Bureau at 1-866-248-3049 or visit our website at www.simonspeakers.com.

Cover designed by Jessica Handelman

Interior designed by Mike Rosamilia

The text of this book was set in Dante MT.

Manufactured in the United States of America 0719 QVE

2 4 6 8 10 9 7 5 3

This book has been cataloged with the Library of Congress.

ISBN 978-1-4814-6032-3 (hc)

ISBN 978-1-4814-6031-6 (pbk)

ISBN 978-1-4814-6033-0 (eBook)

For anyone who has ever felt like a sore thumb
in a room full of pretty pinkies:
This one is for you.

And for the Journey Girls:
Annie Chin
Carrie Diggs
Ruth Gallo
Cara Lane
Sarah Mahieu

Every girl in the world deserves friends
as amazing as you five.

CONTENTS

TOAD GIRL

The bracelet and the first charm appeared the day I punched Austin Jackson in the nose. I didn't mean to slug him. His face just got in my way. It was a bruising end to a disastrous first month in middle school.

You know that kid in class that everyone secretly (and not-so-secretly) thinks is weird? The one people laugh and point at behind their back, the one who gets picked last in gym class, the one you wish you hadn't gotten stuck with for a science partner?

At Dandelion Middle School, that kid is me, Izzy "Don't Call Me Isabella" Malone.

Truthfully, my slide into loserdom started in elementary

school and was pretty much an established fact by the time sixth grade started last month. It's partly because my mouth often has a mind of its own. But I think it's also because there are a bazillion other things I'd rather do than talk about boys, clothes, and makeup, and I refuse to wear strappy sandals and short skirts.

(If you ever catch me wearing strappy sandals or a short skirt, you have my permission to kick my butt.)

I *do* like skirts, though. Really long, colorful ones I get from Dandelion Thrift. I like to wear them with my camouflage combat boots.

I call the look Camohemian.

"I don't understand how it could be locked," Ms. Harmer, my English teacher said, tugging on the door of our classroom. "Fifteen minutes ago it was open."

"Does this mean class is cancelled?" I asked. Our class was held in an outdoor portable. The day was chilly but sunny, and being stuck indoors writing another round of horrible haikus was the last thing I wanted to do.

"No, Isabella—"

"Izzy," I said.

"—that is definitely *not* what that means. Everyone wait here while I go to the teacher's lounge to look for my keys. Lauren, you're in charge while I'm gone."

Lauren Wilcox smiled, all angelic-like. "I will." After Ms. Harmer left, Lauren's smile pulled back, like a beast baring its fangs. "You heard her. *I'm* in charge."

Students clumped off into their cliques. Being the class outcast, I am thoroughly cliqueless, and normally I'd sit by myself. But today I was planning to change all that.

Lauren and her friends claimed a grassy patch of sunlight—kicking out a couple other girls who'd gotten there first. I stared at them and squared my shoulders, preparing myself to do some major strappy-sandal smooching up. Lauren and her crew are the sixth-grade members of the Dandelion Paddlers, a competitive after-school rowing club. Lauren's family owns the aquatic center on Dandelion Lake, and you need to get in good with Lauren if you want to be a Paddler.

I learned that the hard way last summer during Paddler tryouts. I thought the fact that I was a great rower would be enough. There were four open spots, and they all went to Lauren's friends—even though I came in fourth during the timed heats. The last spot went to Stella Franklin, who had somehow managed to become BFFs with Lauren over the summer. I'm guessing the fact that Stella can kiss butt faster than a frog can catch flies has something to do with it.

But I wasn't about to give up. Being on the Paddlers is a big deal in Dandelion Hollow; when my dad was my age he was on the boys' team. He's taken me rowing for years, and we trained for tryouts all summer. Dandelion Lake is my favorite place in the world. I love being on the open water, where the only thing I feel is the wind in my hair, and words like "odd" and "strange" blow away like dead leaves on a blustery autumn day.

Lauren's locker is right next to mine, and this morning I took an extra-long time loading up my backpack so I could listen while she told her friends they were one Paddler short since Emily Harris moved away last week. I figured now was my chance.

"Hi," I said, plunking down next to Lauren. "It's weird Ms. Harmer can't find her keys, right?" I took the headphones from my iPod out of my skirt pocket and twirled them around, like I was bored and just making conversation.

Lauren blinked at me like I was a species she didn't recognize.

"Um, excuse me," Stella Franklin said. "What makes you think you can just sit here?"

It's a free country, is what I wanted to say. "I want to join you" is what I blurted instead.

"*You* want to join *us*?" said another of Lauren's friends. A husky blond girl who was wearing a chunky red headband over her ponytail.

"I mean, I want to join the Paddlers." I looked at Lauren. "I know you have an open spot, and last summer at tryouts I finished ahead of her." I jabbed my finger at Stella, who swelled up like a puffer fish.

"You did not! We tied."

"Nope," I said, twirling my headphones. "I beat you by three-tenths of a second."

Lauren leaned back and looked me up and down. I sat up straight, trying to appear taller. I'm pretty short, but what I lack in size I make up for in won't-quit-till-I-die persistence.

"I only have winners on my team," she said.

"I'm a winner," I said. Only my voice squeaked a little, and "winner" came out "wiener."

"Did you just call yourself a wiener?" Headband Girl asked.

Everyone laughed, and I counted silently to ten, because my patience was all puckered out.

"I think if you saw me paddle again," I said, crossing my legs, "then you'd realize I'm much better than—"

"What are *those*?" Stella interrupted, poking at my combat boots. "Those are the ugliest things I've ever seen. Don't you know boys don't like to get up close and personal with girls who wear boots like that?" She poked me again.

"You keep running your mouth," I snapped, smacking her hand away, "and these boots will get up close and personal with your face."

Darn it! The mouth strikes again!

Lauren directed her gaze to Headband Girl, who seemed to take it as a silent command. She snatched away my headphones and flung them in the air. They circled once in the breeze before landing on an overhanging branch of a nearby tree. Then, one by one, Lauren, Stella, Headband, and the rest of them stood up and left in a line of ponytail-swinging nastiness, leaving me sitting alone, while the rest of the class watched me, waiting to see what I would do.

Yeah, stuff like this is pretty much why I think middle school stinks.

Let's just pause for a moment to consider my options. I could:

> a. cry, which would only convince them I
>   didn't belong on their team.
> b. kick Headband's butt into the next
>   county. (Or try to, anyway. It's hard to

         appear threatening to someone who has
         biceps the size of Nebraska.)
     c. get my headphones back.

Here's the key to surviving as a middle school out-cast: Pretend you don't care. Pretend you have such great self-esteem that everything just rolls off your back. Most important:

Don't show weakness. Ever.

I chose option C. I have a thing for trees, and I'd wanted to climb this particular one for a while. I eat lunch under it every day, on account of the fact that the cafeteria usually smells like burnt burritos.

Plus, it's not like I have anyone to eat with, anyway.

I stood up and stretched. A skip, a hop, and a shimmy later, I was scrambling up the trunk.

"Go, Izzy!" shouted Austin Jackson, who, at the moment, still had a bruise-free face. A few other kids started cheering; Lauren and the Paddlers were already forgotten.

See what I mean? Pretend you don't care. Works like a charm.

I braced my hands against the rough trunk. The star-shaped leaves were the color of a fiery peach, and they whispered in the breeze. The air smelled sharp and crisp, like shiny red apples, and I breathed deep, enjoying being a little bit closer to the sky.

"Toad Girl is crazy," Stella was saying down below. I pretended not to hear. I also pretended I didn't know that was what most of the kids at Dandelion Middle called me. Stella the Terrible and I went to elementary school together and she gave me the nickname at her fourth-grade slumber party, when I put a toad in her sleeping bag. (I swear, that girl can howl like a werewolf on a full moon.)

I hadn't meant to do it. I just got bored watching everyone else test out Stella's lip gloss collection, and I started playing with her brother's sand toad, Count Croakula. I guess I must have lost him. But Stella swore up and down I'd done it on purpose, so I wasn't invited to her birthday party last year. I wasn't invited to a lot of birthday parties last year.

Turns out, most girls would rather put on lip gloss than play with sand toads.

"Come down from there! You'll get us all in trouble!" Stella was now standing under the tree. Lauren must have dispatched her to keep me in line. "Come on. Ms. Harmer will be back any minute."

"Leave Izzy to her solitary pursuits," said Violet Barnaby, who liked to use fancy words. She was sitting off to the side by herself, scribbling in a glittery purple journal. "Ms. Harmer won't find her keys in the teachers' lounge."

"How do you know that?" Stella demanded.

"Because I have them right here." Violet produced a key ring and jingled it.

The class gave a collective gasp, as Violet was known for being an A student who never got in trouble. I took the opportunity to climb up the branch. Slowly, I inched my way across it, where my headphones dangled in the breeze.

"Hey, Toad Girl!" called Tyler Jones. "Think fast!"

He lobbed an orange at me. It missed by a few feet and Austin said, "Tyler, you moron! Get out from under there. . . . I said, *Get Out!*"

"Ouch! All right, all right. I'm going!"

I kept inching forward, and stretched my fingers out to get the headphones. From up here I had a good view of several clusters of maple trees, which in late September were all colored in shades of gold and red and orange. A part of me wished I could stay up here forever, away from the middle school mean girls, who circled like sharks below me. I picked a few leaves and stuck them in my pocket, so I could paste them into my leaf collection later.

"What's going on?" came Ms. Harmer's voice. "Is someone up there?"

Startled, I lost my balance and fell. I caught myself on the branch and swung—gymnast style—through the air, landing right in front of Ms. Harmer.

"Ta-da!" I said, throwing my hands in the air.

A few kids applauded, but Ms. Harmer's face turned purple. "Go to the office. Now!"

As I walked away, I heard Stella say, "Excuse me, Ms. Harmer? You should probably send Violet to the office too. After all, she's the one who stole your keys."

CHAPTER 2

STICKS AND STONES

Coco Martin, my guidance counselor, was unimpressed with my daredevil skills. She tossed me a tube of ointment and a box of Band-Aids. "Clean yourself up," she said, gesturing to some cuts and scrapes on my arms. Then she went back to decorating her office for the fall. On her desk sat piles of tiny pumpkins and colorful ears of corn.

"Someone's grouchy today," I said, rubbing ointment onto my elbow. "Can't you be a little nicer?"

Coco grunted and stuck a pumpkin on her bookcase. "Consider yourself lucky. The only reason you're not in Principal Chilton's office right now is because Ms. Harmer decided stealing keys is a bigger offense than climbing trees. . . . And how many more times am I going to have to tell you not to put your feet up on my desk?"

"I don't know," I said. "How many more times do you think I'll get sent to your office?"

"That's a mystery to me. You've only been here a month, and I think you already hold the school record. It's been—what?—two days since I last saw you? When you kicked Tyler Jones in the shin."

"*That* was totally not my fault. Tyler called me a weirdo and a waste of space."

"'Sticks and stones may break my bones, but names can never hurt me.' It's a saying," Coco said. "Ever heard of it?"

"You know what? Now that you mention it, I think I have!" I nearly sprained my eyeballs, I was trying so hard not to roll them. Words are a weapon, and rotten kids like Tyler Jones get a free pass when it comes to using them, because the marks they leave are invisible. Why don't more adults realize that?

"Tyler trips me every day in class," I pointed out. "He just never gets caught. He hates being my science partner."

"Be that as it may, you need to stop showing up in my office. . . . You know, your sister spent three whole years here, and I don't think I ever even met her."

"Right," I said, feeling the familiar twinge I got whenever Carolyn the Great was mentioned. "But you know your day is always more interesting when me and my sparkling personality make an appearance in it."

Coco pressed her lips together, like she was trying not to smile. "Maybe so. *But*,"—her voice became stern—"sparkling personality or not, I still have to send a note home. School policy and all."

Coco scribbled on the incident report form I was intimately acquainted with and handed it to me just as the bell rang. "Have your parents sign this and bring it back to me," she said.

"I know the drill," I answered, shoving the note into my skirt pocket.

On the walk home from school I passed Violet, who lives in my neighborhood. Violet and I used to be best friends, the kind that played together at lunch and every day after school in my treehouse. Sometimes we'd pretend we were secret CIA agents, or sometimes we'd throw sand at each other and pretend it was fairy dust. But after Violet's mom got sick, and especially after Mrs. Barnaby passed away, Violet never wanted to play.

I considered slowing down to say hi, but Violet was hunched forward, her red peacoat fluttering in the wind as she stomped through a pile of fallen leaves. She didn't look like she wanted company. I bet she'd gotten into a heap load of trouble for stealing Ms. Harmer's keys, and I felt a little bad, because maybe Stella wouldn't have told on her if I hadn't climbed the tree.

I sped up and came upon a group of kids who were laughing. "Hey, Toad Girl!" a boy said as I passed. "Caught any flies lately?" Something small pinged off my shoulder.

"Dude, she *looks* like a toad," said another boy, as everyone laughed. "Ribbit, ribbit."

Sticks and stones, I told myself.

I felt the ping again and saw a yellow candy corn bounce off my arm and onto the ground—they were throwing them at me. I picked it up and yelled, "Thanks for the snack!" before popping it in my mouth and running ahead.

3

BRIGHT STARS
AND CLEAR SKIES

As soon as I got home I headed for the kitchen. Mom was sitting at the table; she had an iced coffee in one hand and her cell phone in the other, pressed close to her ear. "Yes, I understand," she was saying, "but Kendra Franklin has never been the business-friendly sort, has she? If you support my campaign and I'm elected, I promise that will change."

Mom has run just about every fund-raiser in Dandelion Hollow; I guess it was just a matter of time before she decided she should become mayor and run the whole town. The only problem is that Dandelion Hollow has a really popular long-serving mayor: Kendra Franklin,

Stella the Terrible's mother. Mom and Mayor Franklin went to middle and high school together. They didn't like each other much way back then, but now their relationship is iceberg cold. The election is in early November, and so far, things aren't looking all that great for Mom.

Before I could make a quick getaway with the bag of cookies I grabbed from the pantry, Mom glanced at me and tucked the phone under her ear. "Hold it right there, Isabella. Why are your arms all scratched up?"

"Izzy."

"What?"

"Izzy. You know I hate the name Isabella."

"Fine. Why are your arms all scratched up, *Izzy*?"

"I fell out of a tree."

"You fell out of a tree? Lovely. How many people saw you walking around town looking like this?"

By "people," Mom actually means "potential voters."

"It happened during my last class, and then I came straight home. Relax—I doubt it's going to cost you the election."

"Watch your tone, young lady. Exactly how did you manage to fall out of a tree during class time?"

I handed her Coco's note. "That should cover it."

Mom scanned the note, and the lines on her forehead

deepened into canals. "We'll talk about this later," she hissed. She put the phone back up to her ear and turned away. "I understand your concern, but I think if the Wild-flower Society could see their way to supporting me . . ."

I left the kitchen and went upstairs to Carolyn's room—I mean, Carolyn's and my room. Grandma Bertie and my great-aunt Mildred both live with us, and since the two of them can barely go five minutes without fighting, they each have to have their own room. Aunt Mildred has my room now, and I share with Carolyn. But Carolyn's room had already been filled to bursting with her piano and her guitar collection, which meant I had to shove a lot of my things in the attic. Aunt Mildred says I can come visit her and my old room any time I want, but it's just not the same.

I maneuvered around all Carolyn's stuff and settled down on my bed with my cookies and backpack. Then I pulled out my textbooks. The teachers at Dandelion Middle like to give out buckets of homework—as if I don't have anything better to do after sitting in class all day. My policy is, I do just enough to get by. But I figured Mom would be on a rampage after reading Coco's note, so I decided to complete all my assignments.

Call it a charitable act on my part.

After I finished—several hours later, when I swear my eyeballs were beginning to sweat—I left my room and headed for the back door. I had to watch my step as I zigzagged through the backyard. My dad is an amateur grower of giant pumpkins, and the yard was taken over by humongous orange gourds that each weighed hundreds of pounds.

After I stepped around our largest pumpkin, an Atlantic Giant we named Bozo, I reached my treehouse. It was the one place where I felt like I could be completely alone in my crowded house. And it had a great view of the sky.

Bright stars and clear skies: Those are the things I like to stare at most.

The sky tonight was clear with a million glittering stars winking in the moonlight as I climbed the ladder to the treehouse. Clear enough to give me a good view of Orion and the Big Dipper—my two best friends so far in the sixth grade.

"Hello, Orion. Nice to see you tonight, Big D," I said, leaning out the window. "Today I got in trouble in Ms. Harmer's class."

My two best friends said nothing as I told them about my day, but that's what I always liked about talking to the stars. They were good listeners and they were a lot easier to understand than the girls at Dandelion Middle.

The opening strains of Beethoven's "Moonlight Sonata" floated from the house. Carolyn must be home from her piano lesson, practicing already. She was playing it in her recital tomorrow night, and I was pretty sure she'd picked it because I told her I liked to listen to it while I stared at the stars. I spread my arms and pretended I was conducting, and that Orion and Big D were my audience.

After I finished I rummaged through the boxes I kept in the treehouse, pulled out a large packet of star stickers—the kind that glow in the dark—and began sticking them on the walls. They come in handy on the nights when you can't see the real stars. I took my time sticking them on—the backs are really sticky, so once you stick them somewhere, they aren't coming off.

"Isabella, dinner's ready!" Mom called.

"Izzy!" I shouted back. I stuck on one last sticker then started down the ladder.

In the kitchen, Mom and Dad sat at either end of the table. Dad was still wearing his uniform. He's the town's police chief, but since nothing much ever happens in Dandelion Hollow, most of his calls are about missing cats or teenagers toilet-papering houses. Both he and Mom were sitting ramrod straight, so I could tell they'd been discussing Coco's note.

Carolyn and I sat on one side, and Grandma Bertie and Aunt Mildred sat on the other. When we were all settled, Aunt Mildred sniffed her bowl and said, "Janine, what on earth did you do to this chili?"

"Don't sass my daughter," Grandma Bertie said. "Without her, you'd be out on the street on your hind end."

"Don't sass *me*, Bertha," Aunt Mildred shot back. "If Janine expects us to eat, she needs to concoct something that doesn't make your sinuses run."

Grandma Bertie and Aunt Mildred are twins. They're so alike they have the same wrinkles, even though they've lived completely different lives. The only way you can tell them apart is by the expression on their face. Grandma Bertie's eyes usually sparkle, while Aunt Mildred always looks like she's just smelled something rotten. Grandma Bertie got married and has lived in Dandelion Hollow all her life, but up until a couple months ago Aunt Mildred spent about forty years living in Europe—mostly Paris—and she never married. She says it's because she never understood what all the fuss was about children and husbands. But Grandma Bertie says it's because no man ever liked taking his coffee and eggs with a side of pickled prunes.

The last time Grandma Bertie said that, our family was actually eating eggs, and Aunt Mildred threw hers. They splatted on Grandma Bertie's earlobe. Then Dad mouthed the words *senior center* at Mom, but his whisper was more of an irritated rasp. After that, Aunt Mildred and Grandma Bertie made up real fast. But nobody talked to Dad for the rest of the day.

"I used a little too much red pepper, but you can put sour cream in it to tone it down," Mom said.

Aunt Mildred muttered something under her breath. She was probably cussing in French again. Mom doesn't tolerate cussing in any language, but since she doesn't speak French she's never exactly sure what Aunt Mildred is saying. "So, everyone," Grandma Bertie said in a bright voice, "how was your day?"

"Rotten," Mom said, stabbing at her salad. "I spent two hours on the phone with the president of the Wildflower Society, only for her to tell me at the end they're still supporting Kendra Franklin."

"That's terrible, dear," Grandma Bertie said, exchanging glances with Aunt Mildred. "But remember what we talked about? Being positive? Someone tell me the *best part* of your day."

I stuck a large spoonful of chili in my mouth so I didn't

have to answer. The best part of my day was that Tyler didn't try to trip me in science class—he was probably afraid I'd kick him again.

"Come on," Grandma Bertie prompted. "Carolyn, you first."

Carolyn swallowed a bite of chili. "I have two best parts. Miss Collins says I'm ready for the recital tomorrow night."

Of course she was ready for the recital. Carolyn is a musical genius, and everyone knows one day she'll leave town for a bigger city with brighter lights. Mom is hoping for San Francisco, since that's only a few hours southwest of Dandelion Hollow. But Carolyn wants to attend Juilliard, some performing arts school in New York. For now, though, the stage at Dandelion High will have to be enough.

"The other part is that I got a pumpkin-gram today."

Pumpkin-grams are a big fall tradition at Dandelion High where kids pay a dollar to write a special note on an orange construction-paper pumpkin and have it sent to their friends.

"Was it from a boy?" Grandma Bertie's eyes went wide. "I'll bet it was, wasn't it?"

"Horse rubbish!" Aunt Mildred said, brandishing her

spoon. "Carolyn is far too young to be receiving pumpkin-grams from boys."

"Have you forgotten Scooter McGee?" Grandma Bertie said, batting her eyes. "I seem to recall he once sent *you* a pumpkin-gram."

"Check your memory, Bertha. That old fool gave me a flower on Valentine's Day—they didn't even *have* pumpkin-grams back in our day. And we were in eleventh grade; Carolyn's only in ninth."

"It was from Layla," Carolyn said. Layla was Carolyn's best friend, but since Layla had gotten back together with her boyfriend, Carolyn hadn't seen her that much recently. Personally, I felt like Carolyn was lucky just to *have* a best friend.

"That sounds lovely, Carolyn," Mom said, smiling. Her smile tightened, though, when Grandma Bertie said, "What about you, Izzy? What was the best part of your day?"

"I didn't have one," I said, and stuck another large bite in my mouth.

"Well, I can't imagine that you would," Mom said. "Seeing as how you got sent to the office again."

And there it was. When it comes to family dinners, Mom can go from praising our accomplishments (always

Carolyn's) to lamenting our screw-ups (always mine) in zero seconds flat.

Everyone was silent. Carolyn concentrated on her chili, but underneath the table she reached over and squeezed my hand.

Dad shot Mom a wary look, and Grandma Bertie said, "Janine, dear, I don't think now is the time to—"

"Stay out of it, Mother," Mom said. "Stop telling me how to parent my daughter. You know I hate it when you do that." She turned to me. "Well? Do you have anything you want to say?"

"Not really," I answered, which I thought was a perfectly acceptable and honest answer, but Mom and Dad both looked annoyed.

"I don't see what all the fuss is about," Aunt Mildred said. "I got sent to the principal's office all the time when I was Izzy's age. If you ask me—"

"No one did, dear," Grandma Bertie said.

"But if they *did*," Aunt Mildred said, shooting Grandma Bertie a dirty look, "I'd say everyone is overreacting. It was just a tree. Doesn't anyone climb them anymore?"

"That's not the point," Dad said. "The point is, Izzy keeps getting into trouble, and so far nothing we've done seems to be making any difference." He sighed and pushed his plate away. "Izzy—your mother and I really don't know what to do. We've grounded you, banned electronics, sent you to your room, and these things are still getting sent home." He held up the note from Coco. "I doubt taking your iPod away again is going to change anything."

Dad has always made it clear that, as the chief of police, he expects his daughters to behave like Respectable People. This isn't a problem for Carolyn the Great, musical prodigy extraordinaire. But compared to her and my civic-minded parents, I often feel like an emerging juvenile delinquent.

"Right." Mom nodded. "So we've been exploring more creative options."

"Creative options?" I repeated. "What does *that* mean?"

"It means we've been looking into a few things, and last week we decided to do something unconventional." Mom paused. "We signed you up for charm school."

Charm school? Me? Had they lost their minds?

I snorted. "Um . . . I don't think I'm charm school material."

"That's exactly the point." Dad crossed his arms, and his police badge flashed in the light. "We're really concerned. And with your mother's campaign . . ."

He didn't finish his sentence. He didn't have to. With election day creeping closer, Mom wanted to project the image of a family who has it all together, and right now I was messing everything up.

Just last week a photographer came to the house to take a family picture for Mom's new campaign mailers. He said we should go for the all-American look. Then he frowned at me and suggested I change my clothes, and, if it wasn't too much trouble, could I do something about my hair, too?

I told Mom "all-American" should mean I have the freedom to wear whatever I wanted without anyone getting on my case about it. But apparently, that's not how politics actually work. So I changed my clothes, tied my hair in a ponytail, and faked a smile. The mailers were supposed to be ready any day now, but I wasn't in any hurry to see them.

"Now, I'm not able to drive you to a proper charm school," Mom said, which was just a fancy way of saying she was too busy to be bothered. "So we signed you up for a home-study course."

"O-*kay*. What am I supposed to do for this home-study course?"

"You have to . . . well, I don't remember exactly." She

frowned. "A flier came for it in the mail last week. The name of the school is Mrs. Whippie's—"

Grandma Bertie started choking on her chili. Aunt Mildred jumped up and began pounding on her back until she hawked a huge chili-scented loogie across the table; it landed in the salad bowl.

"Nice one," Carolyn said.

"Mildred! You nearly broke my ribs!" Grandma Bertie yelled when she could speak again.

"You were choking," Aunt Mildred said. "Next time should I sit back and do nothing?"

Dad and Mom glanced at each other. "Anyway . . ." From under the table Mom produced a chunky cream envelope. "Your first assignment came in the mail today."

"No way," I said. "I am not joining some stupid charm school."

"Yes, you are," Dad said. "Otherwise, you can forget about Pumpkin Palooza, and racing in the regatta. Do I make myself clear?"

CHAPTER

4

MRS. WHIPPIE'S
EARN YOUR
CHARM SCHOOL

One great thing about combat boots: They can make a lot of noise. Mine drummed a booming chorus as I stomped up the stairs after dinner. I went to my bedroom and rummaged through my dresser for my workout gear. My arms and legs needed to burn off some energy before my mouth got me in trouble.

Pumpkin Palooza is Dandelion Hollow's annual harvest festival. It's always held the Saturday before Halloween at Caulfield Farm. There are games, prizes, and food, but the biggest attraction is the Great Pumpkin Regatta, where pumpkins weighing hundreds of pounds are hollowed out and turned into small boats and raced across the Caulfields' large pond.

This year Dad is letting me race Bozo in the regatta. Dad says he's happy to do it; for the last two years Mike Harrison, from Harrison's Hardware, has won, and Dad says he's just plain tired of hearing him brag about his superior pumpkins. I think I've got a good shot at winning; I've been working out on the rowing machine in our garage every night for two months. As motivation, I just visualize the shiny pumpkin trophy and the five-hundred-dollar check they give to the winner.

I'm not sure what I'd do with the money—maybe I'd buy a kayak of my own—but I definitely plan to put the trophy on the same shelf where Mom displays all of the awards Carolyn has won from her voice and piano recitals. Plus, I want Lauren and the other Paddlers to see how good I am.

So if there was anything Dad could say to get me to do this dumb charm school course, telling me I couldn't compete in the regatta was it.

After I changed into my sweats, I headed for the garage. I sat down at the rowing machine and looked at the envelope Dad gave me. My name and address were written in the middle; the return address was a PO Box in San Francisco. As soon as I ripped the top off, the scent of roses and cream wafted into the air. Inside, besides a folded-up piece of velvety stationery, sat a gold chain-link bracelet and a tiny envelope charm, the kind with a clasp to attach to the bracelet. The envelope charm was a rose-gold color, and the top of it actually flipped open. This was already the strangest letter I'd ever received, and things just got stranger when I opened it and read, sneezing a couple times from the rosy perfume:

Dear Isabella,

Congratulations! You've just been enrolled in Mrs. Whippie's Earn Your Charm School. In order to complete my course, you must perform a series of tasks. Charms to put on your bracelet will accompany each task. The first task: Write a nice letter to someone who could use some cheering up. Then you will have earned an envelope charm, and you may place it on your bracelet. More tasks and charms will follow. Complete them all, and you will have earned your charm, and you will also have earned a prize unlike any other. Please send me a letter letting me know you've completed your first task.

I reread the letter a second time. A prize unlike any other? What did that mean? Weren't charm schools supposed to teach manners and all sorts of fancy things? I had never heard of earning charms to put on a bracelet before.

A loud *thud* sounded on the garage door, followed by, "Izzy? Are you in there?"

Austin Jackson lived next door and had the same homework philosophy as I did, which left us plenty of time to shoot hoops in his driveway. Austin and I don't usually talk at school. It's like an unofficial rule that we mostly ignore each other all day and then wait until after dinner to hang out. I'm not sure why; that's just the way it is.

I put the letter and the bracelet on top of the washing machine, then pressed the garage door switch. As soon as it had rolled halfway up, Austin ducked under and came inside.

"Are you training for the regatta tonight?" After I nodded he said, "Take a break. You know you want to lose to me in a half-court game."

I rolled my eyes but followed him over to his driveway anyways. Austin used to be the shortest kid in our class, but he had shot up over the summer, so now we were about equal height. This had a tendency to make him think he was a lot cooler than he actually was.

"So your big plan is to win the regatta and hope that Lauren Wilcox and the rest of them are so impressed they'll let you join the Paddlers?" Austin asked, dribbling the ball. After I nodded again, he said, "Okay, but . . . you know that's totally weird, right?"

I shrugged; it wasn't like I'd never been called "weird" before, and besides, not many people saw racing a gigantic pumpkin as the answer to their problems. Also, I didn't want to tell him that sometimes when I trained I imagined myself competing in a race while Mom sat on the sidelines, loudly telling anyone who'd listen how I was a second-generation Paddler and how proud she was of me. Besides, I really *had* beaten Stella at tryouts over the summer, and I should have been on the team already. I figured they just needed a little reminder.

"It's on," Austin said, tossing me the ball. "Prepare yourself for imminent humiliation."

"Prepare *yourself.* You're the one who always loses."

I dribbled the ball to the edge of the sidewalk, our starting line. I stepped in and Austin planted himself in front of me, hands out front to block my vision. "Let's see what you've got," he said.

I faked right and sprinted past him. The basketball sailed through the hoop. *Swish!*

"I let you have that," he said, dribbling the ball back to the sidewalk. "I just wanted to make sure you got on the board."

"Sure you did," I said.

He stepped in and faked right, then left. As I turned back to sprint left he bumped into me, sending me flying until I smacked the concrete. I groaned and sat up. My knees throbbed and my palms stung.

"Izzy, are you okay?" Austin dropped the ball and held out his hand. The minute I grasped it and stood up, a strange buzzing feeling went through me, and I could feel my cheeks heating up.

"Are you okay?" he repeated, glancing down at my knees. "You're bleeding."

"I'm fine," I snapped, wishing he would stop looking at my legs. "A little blood never hurt anyone." I yanked my hand out of his, but the buzzing feeling didn't go away. I looked down and dusted myself off.

We took a break a while later (after I'd won the first game, I'd like to point out), and Austin said, "Nice work today, climbing the tree. The Hammer looked like she was going to explode." "The Hammer" was what everyone called Ms. Harmer behind her back.

"Yeah," I said, "but my mom is pretty upset about it." I

dribbled the ball a few times. "She signed me up for some weird charm school."

"Charm school? *You?*" Austin looked incredulous.

"Yes. *Me*," I said, and he began to laugh. "What's so funny?"

"Your mother would have more luck winning her election than teaching you how to be charming. Izzy Malone, going to charm school! Are you going to walk across the room with a book stuck on your head?"

"No, it's not like that at all," I said as he doubled over with laughter. "And I really don't see what's so funny."

"It's just that"—he gasped—"it would be like teaching a hippo to wear high heels!"

Bam!

In my defense, I'd like to say I truly didn't mean to punch him in the face. I just meant to give him a little hey-you're-being-totally-lame shove. But he was still crouched over, shaking with laughter, and right then was when he decided to look up.

"Ow! Geez, Izzy, what'd you do that for?"

"I can be just as charming as the next girl," I snapped. Then I stalked away, leaving him to wipe up his bloody nose.

CATCHING
FLIES

The next morning, Mrs. Jackson called and told Mom I'd assaulted her son. Mom nearly choked on her iced coffee and said I'd better apologize to Austin, pronto.

"But it was an accident. I wasn't trying to—"

"I really don't want to hear your excuses today, Isabella." Mom picked up her keys and slung her gym bag over her shoulder. "You can walk to school. I have an early campaign meeting with the members of the Rotary Club and then Zumba afterward." Zumba is this aerobics class where she and a bunch of other moms jump around and pretend they're teenagers at a dance party. She takes it pretty seriously—I once saw her in the garage practicing her moves.

I thought about it on the way to school, and figured that since I needed to write a letter to earn Mrs. Whippie's envelope charm anyway, I'd give Austin a handwritten apology. That way I'd kill two birds with one stone, as Grandma Bertie likes to say. While I was in science class and Mr. Webber was droning on about acids and bases and pH—which made me think of a deodorant commercial—I tried writing him a note:

Dear Austin,
I'm sorry your face got in my way. Next time, please move faster.

Dear Austin,
Your nose wouldn't be bloody if you were just a few inches taller. You might want to work on that.

Dear Austin,
I'm sorry I hurt your nose. My hand doesn't hurt at all, though. I think we can both agree this means I'm tougher than you are.

Dear Austin,
I wouldn't have shoved you if you weren't being so lame.

I wadded up another piece of paper. When it came down to it, I couldn't think of a good written apology that wouldn't get me in more trouble. I figured that meant I'd have to give him a garden-variety verbal one. At lunch I found him eating in the cafeteria with Tyler Jones and Trent Walker. For some reason, I felt nervous approaching him, but I didn't know why. It was just Austin, after all.

"Hi, Austin."

He stood up quickly, before I could sit down. "What do you want?" he said.

I looked at him. Slightly *up* at him. Had he grown another inch overnight? Also, why hadn't I ever noticed how blue his eyes were before? Blue and really bright, like the sky on a clear day. "Um . . . I just wanted to say I'm sorry for—"

"It's all good." He smiled tightly and lowered his voice. "I told my mom it was just an accident."

"No, really, my mom is on my case and she won't get off until I properly apologize."

"Apologize?" Tyler piped up. "For what?"

"For punching Austin in the face last night," I said.

"Punching him?" Tyler laughed. "Dude, you told us you walked into a door. . . . Hey, everyone! Austin got punched by a girl!"

"Whatever." I could never figure out why Austin hung out with those idiots. "Anyway, I just wanted to say I was—"

"Sorry," Austin said through gritted teeth. "Got it."

"Austin got his butt whipped by Toad Girl!" Tyler shouted, and Trent laughed so hard milk snorted from his nostrils.

The nearby tables went silent. "Ribbit, ribbit!" someone called.

Austin stared down at the floor, his cheeks flamed with color, and when he looked up at me, his eyes had hardened. "Go back to your lily pad," he said, loud enough for everyone nearby to hear. "I didn't see any flies on the menu today, Toad Girl."

My mouth opened in a perfect O—just wide enough to catch all those flies.

Then I turned and ran.

It was raining, so instead of heading for the tree next to English class I went to my backup spot, the hallway outside the library. I liked to sit there because on one of the walls there were small sections of peeling gray paint. The paint underneath was orange, and I always wondered whoever in their right mind thought it was a smart idea to cover it with a boring gray color.

I settled down against the wall and promised myself I wouldn't cry. I had thought Austin and I were just after-school friends because we didn't have any classes together besides English, and we didn't hang out with the same people. (Well, *I* didn't hang out with *any* people.) But was it something else? Was Austin *embarrassed* to be my friend?

A little while later, the bell rang, and I glanced at the gray wall one last time. As I headed off to my next class, it dawned on me that in a drab place like Dandelion Middle, maybe there just wasn't any room for a color as bright as orange.

CHAPTER 6

EARNING CHARM

By the time Carolyn's recital rolled around later that night, I still hadn't written a nice note to anyone. I'd been so upset over Austin that I hadn't thought much about it. In the backseat of Mom's car on the way to Dandelion High, I turned the envelope charm over and over in my hand, hoping inspiration would strike. But the truth was, I couldn't think of a single person who'd want a note from Toad Girl.

"I'm nervous," Carolyn whispered as we got out of the car, and I knew she was about to engage in her ritual pre-performance freak-out.

"You're going to be fantastic," I said.

"I'm going to throw up," she said.

"You're going to go out there and show everyone how great you are. Because you are Carolyn the Great." In these moments, I always feel like I'm the older sister.

"I'm not great. I'm awful. Really, really terrible."

"Well," I said finally, "I wasn't gonna say anything, but now that you mention it . . . you're right: You're terrible. Would you like me to perform tonight instead?"

Carolyn laughed and wrapped her arm around me. "Thanks, Izzy," she whispered. "I don't know what I'd do without you."

"You'd be fine," I said. "Except your life would be a lot more boring."

As soon as we walked inside the auditorium at Dandelion High, Mom went bounding toward a cluster of well-dressed, overperfumed ladies—they were all members of her book club. A few of the women exchanged side glances, and I wondered how much they actually liked Mom.

Now that I thought about it, a couple girls in my history class had given each other that same look this morning when I was assigned to their small group.

"I seriously can't handle the book club ladies tonight," Carolyn murmured.

"Want me to run interference for you?" I asked, and she nodded.

"Janine, what a wonderfully talented daughter you have," said one book club lady.

"Thank you so much," I said loudly, stepping in front of them while Carolyn slipped around and headed backstage. "I *am* wonderful, aren't I? But talented? That's debatable."

"Ah yes, well . . ." The book club lady looked momentarily flummoxed, before turning away from me. "Janine, how is the campaign coming along?"

I left Mom and the other ladies and found our seats. It seemed nearly half of Dandelion Hollow had come out tonight. Violet and her dad were settling into a row to my left. The concert began a few minutes later, and one high schooler after another took the stage to sing, or play the piano or some other musical instrument. But I could tell that most of the audience was waiting. It was Carolyn's first concert as a high school freshman, and everyone in town had been hearing for years about the chief of police's musical prodigy daughter.

Finally, it was Carolyn's turn. She sat down at the piano, and a hush fell over the audience as she began to play her selection from Beethoven. Once she finished, she started right in with another song. This one had words; it was a song Carolyn had written herself. She said she just woke up one day and the music and lyrics were floating in her head, like wispy clouds on a spring morning. Her song was as soft as a lullaby but as powerful as a tornado.

While I listened to her perform, I felt like I could cry from the beauty of her voice and how she could take a complicated piano piece and make it appear effortless. That was *my* sister up there, Carolyn the Great.

But all too soon, something changed, and I felt an acidic, green-eyed monster eating at my insides, especially when I glanced at Mom and saw the tears in her eyes, and how she mouthed every word right along with Carolyn. For some reason, I thought about the times I'd begged her to come along when Dad took me rowing, but she was always too busy driving Carolyn to voice, piano, or guitar lessons.

How can you compete with a sister who sang before she could speak, who taught herself to play the piano when she was five, then turned around and taught herself to play the guitar when she was eight? (Mom had a special one made, because Carolyn's hands were too small to hold a regular size.)

The simple answer is: You can't.

I glanced over and saw Violet crying. I remembered it was Violet's mom who gave Carolyn her first piano lesson. The piano in Carolyn's room—*our* room—actually came from the Barnabys. Mr. Barnaby gave it to Carolyn after Mrs. Barnaby died.

I figured if anyone needed a nice note right now, it would be Violet.

I took a wadded-up piece of notebook paper from my coat pocket, grabbed a pen from Mom's purse, and started writing. This time, I knew just what to say:

Dear Violet,

This song reminds me of your mom. I sure do miss her. She was really beautiful. I hope she's in heaven, and that the music the angels make is as pretty as the songs my sister sings. I hope you are enjoying middle school.

P.S.: I thought it was pretty awesome how you stole Ms. Harmer's keys.

Once Carolyn finished, everyone gave her a standing ovation. Then they started filing out of the room for intermission. Violet and Mr. Barnaby stood up; Mr. Barnaby said something about getting some fresh air. Mom was busy with a line of well-wishers (aka potential voters) waiting to congratulate her for having the good sense to give birth to someone as amazing as Carolyn. I excused myself and slipped over to Violet's seat and tucked the letter into the pocket of her peacoat.

I took my bracelet and the envelope charm out of my pocket. "I have earned my charm," I whispered to myself. The overhead lights dimmed, signaling intermission was almost over, and people began returning to their seats. After I hooked the charm on and slid the bracelet onto my wrist, the lights flickered again, and the tiny envelope seemed to illuminate and sparkle. A few minutes later, as I watched Violet curiously dig into her coat pocket and pull out my note, I felt a little lighter.

CHAPTER 7

STAR-SPANGLED SUNSETS

Dear Mrs. Whippie,

I wrote someone a note tonight. Her name is Violet, and we used to be best friends. I watched her read it, and I know it made her smile.

I wish someone would write me a nice note. Sometimes at school I hear kids telling their friends to text them. I don't own a cell phone, but even if I did, there isn't really anyone I could text.

Anyways, I guess that means I have earned my envelope charm. It sure is pretty. It reminds me of the jewelry I sometimes see at Dandelion Thrift. I tried to show the bracelet to my mom tonight after my sister Carolyn's concert, but she was really busy talking to Dandelion High's drama teacher. He offered Carolyn the lead in the school musical. She didn't even have to audition. He said she was so talented the role was hers if she wanted it, which of course she did.

But anyway, go ahead and send me that second charm. So far your school isn't too lame. I thought you'd make me do stupid stuff like walk across the floor in high heels or learn how to properly hold a teacup, which, if you knew me, you'd know that was a lost cause.

Also if you knew me, you'd know most people think I'm strange. Sometimes I feel like in middle school you're only supposed to care about boys, clothes, and makeup, and if you don't, people think you're weird or wild. I guess I just don't understand. I collect leaves, not lip gloss, and I still like climbing trees and splashing in ponds, and sometimes I wish I could fly. I wonder if the stars would look any different if I was just a little closer to the sky.

The other day I was in my treehouse watching the sunset, waiting for the stars to come out, and I swear

the sky was striped reddish and white with blue clouds.
It was like a star-spangled sunset. I thought my mom
would appreciate that, since she's running for mayor of
our town, but when I told her, she just looked at me like
I was speaking a foreign language. I get that look a lot,
actually. Anyway, thanks for the charm.

Your Friend,
Izzy Malone

P.S.: Please don't call me Isabella. That name belongs to
a really pretty girl who never wrecks her clothes and who
never gets dirt under her fingernails. That's definitely
not me. My name is Izzy.

CHAPTER
8
AUTUMN RAINSTORMS

Over the weekend, Dad took me kayaking at Dandelion Lake. He timed me, and sure enough, all my work on the rowing machine was starting to pay off. I practiced till my arms ached so badly I thought they were going to fall off, but when we drove home that afternoon, I was smiling. I was getting faster, and I was pretty sure the next time the Paddlers saw me race, they'd realize I belonged on their team.

A few days later, I was at school sitting under my tree. It was lunchtime, and all around me leaves were fluttering to the ground like a blazing autumn rainstorm. I was examining a couple leaves that looked like they blew in from a different tree. They were thin and oblong, mostly green at the edges, but bright pink in the middle. They reminded me of something. . . .

"Lizard tongues," I whispered, pasting them into the notebook where I kept my leaf collection. "They look like lizard tongues."

"Did your mom tell you to write me a note?"

Startled, I looked up. "What?"

Violet was standing over me, her arms crossed tightly across her chest. Her hair hung down her back in dark brown curls. Her pale skin was flushed from the cold, and her rosy lips were screwed up in a scowl.

"The note you slipped me last week at the concert. Did your mom tell you to do that?"

"No," I said.

"Then why did you write it?"

I had forgotten how bossy Violet could be, and I reminded myself to keep my mouth shut. *We don't know what she's going through*, my mom would always say after Mrs. Barnaby died, when Violet ignored me at school or her dad said she didn't want to come out of the house and play after I'd knocked on her door.

It was true I didn't know what Violet was going through, but what *I* was going through was losing Violet right about the time everyone started calling me Toad Girl. That would have been a great time to have a best friend.

"Well?" She practically tapped her foot while she waited for me to answer.

I never liked it when she bossed me around. "Why do you care?" I countered. "And why aren't you eating in the cafeteria?"

"I loathe the cafeteria. I find it positively revolting, so I usually eat outside the music room." That was Violet for you. It wasn't enough to say she hated the cafeteria. No, she *loathed* it. "And I care because I am sick of everyone being nice to me just because I'm the girl with the dead mother."

I flinched. I'd also forgotten how blunt she could be.

"I sent you the note because I wanted to . . . and because I'm trying to win a prize."

Violet had green eyes with flecks of gold. Those eyes always seemed to hold a question, like she was trying to figure out if you were worth her time or not. And the minute I said the word "prize," her eyes lightened, like she'd decided I was.

"A prize? What kind of prize?"

"Someone sent me a letter telling me I had to send someone else a letter."

"You mean, like a chain letter?"

"No. It's for a charm school, and I have to do all these things to win a prize."

Violet looked thoroughly confused. I knew I wasn't explaining it well, so I held up my wrist. "It has to do with my charm bracelet."

The bell rang then, and Violet said, "That sounds weird . . . but sort of cool." She paused. "What are you doing after school today?"

What was I doing? The same thing I did every day: walking home by myself and trying not to feel like a loser while everyone around me talked to their friends.

"Nothing," I said.

"Want to meet at the Kaleidoscope Café?" Violet glanced at my bracelet. "You could tell me more about it then."

"Sure," I said.

"Cool." She turned to go, then turned back. "By the way, your sister really does have an angelic voice."

Somehow, I knew she was trying to apologize, but I wasn't exactly sure for what.

CHAPTER 9

THE KALEIDOSCOPE CAFÉ

Dandelion Hollow sits at a forgotten edge of Napa Valley, a place that is super popular with tourists. Except we don't have any tourists or hotels. There also aren't any chain restaurants or big banks. The town is just too small. All the businesses are locally owned, including the Kaleidoscope, Dandelion Hollow's only full-service restaurant.

The sky was the color of a polished nickel as I left school and headed down Clover Street to the café. The Kaleidoscope is smack-dab in the middle of downtown Dandelion Hollow, just across from Dandelion Square—a large village green with park benches, a fountain, a gazebo, and a small playground for kids.

The Kaleidoscope was named by Ms. Zubov, the café's owner, because she said she liked the word. But most people said it got its name because the menu was constantly shifting around, and you just never knew exactly what you were gonna get. Usually, it featured whatever Ms. Zubov was harvesting from the large garden she kept out back. Ms. Zubov was hands down the best gardener in Dandelion Hollow. She said it was because the soil in Northern California was a lot easier to work with than the packed earth she grew up with in Russia.

Judging by the smell when I walked into the café, her soil was still serving up plates of her famous Parmesan-and-basil baked tomatoes. I glanced around, wondering if Violet was already here, when I heard, "Psst! Izzy! This way!" In the corner, Violet was sitting by herself in a circular booth that was nearly hidden by a large planter.

"Hi, Violet," I said, sliding in across from her.

"Shhh, keep your voice down." She peeked over the planter, then quickly turned back around.

"Why?" I asked. "Who are you hiding from?"

"Ms. Harmer—she's sitting with Coco Martin over by the jukebox."

I looked over and, sure enough, there they were, sipping coffee and chatting. Just behind them, six old men from the Rotary Club were seated at their usual spots at the counter. One of them, a man wearing wire-rimmed glasses and a gray cap covering white tufty hair raised his voice and said, "Rubbish! Janine Malone will be the best mayor this town's ever seen!" I figured Mom must have won him over in their meeting last week.

"Why did you steal the Hammer's keys, anyway?" I asked. The Violet I knew used to be teacher's pet.

Violet shrugged. "I just wanted out of her class, and that did the trick. I have Miss Carter for English now."

I filed that information away for possible use later. Generally speaking, I don't go looking to cause trouble at school (trouble seems to find me on its own just fine), but it might come in handy knowing that stealing the Hammer's keys was a surefire way to get booted from her class.

"Hello, Izzy," Ms. Zubov said, appearing at our table. "Can you tell your mother I heard from Earl at the post office that her campaign mailers came in today? They should be delivered sometime this afternoon. I told him they could leave them on the back porch and your mom and I will deal with them tomorrow."

"Sure," I said. Ms. Zubov and Grandma Bertie are good friends, and since our house is so crowded, Ms.

Zubov offered to let Mom use her storeroom as a sort of makeshift campaign headquarters.

"Great." She produced a pen and her order pad. "What can I get you girls today?"

"I'll have the baked tomatoes," I said.

"Can't—we ran out a few minutes ago. The specials now are zucchini pasta, zucchini pancakes, and zucchini pizza bites. I'm using up the last of the summer's harvest."

"Why can't you ever make zucchini bread?" Violet complained.

"Don't get smart with me," Ms. Zubov said, tapping Violet on the head with her menu pad. "Are you going to order something, or what?"

"What about hamburgers?" I asked.

"Meat smells putrid to me," Violet said. "Can you order something else? I'm a vegetarian."

"You are?" I hadn't remembered that about Violet, and I wondered when she'd become a vegetarian. It seemed there were a lot of things I didn't know about her now.

After we settled on plates of zucchini fries and Ms. Zubov had left, Violet said, "So . . . someone sent you a letter? Not an e-mail? A real, proper letter . . . like with a stamp and everything?" Violet looked like she couldn't imagine such a thing.

"Yep, a real letter." Briefly, I explained about Mrs. Whippie and her charm school. "Her second letter came in the mail yesterday, along with this." I held up a tiny treasure box charm. It was gold and pink with bits of colored glass inside that looked like gemstones.

Violet took the charm and turned it over in her hands. "My mom used to write me letters," she said wistfully. "She would take all my spelling words and use them in a letter she wrote to me." The wistfulness vanished and she held out her hand. "Show me the letter," she demanded.

I produced the second letter and pushed it across the table. A waitress brought us glasses of water, and I sipped mine while Violet read the letter aloud:

Dear Izzy,

I'm partial to the stars too! Next time I see a star-spangled sunset I'll be sure to think of you. I'm glad you like my course so far. I promise not to give you any tasks you might think are "too lame." As for learning to wear high heels, no need to worry. I've got no tolerance for those dreadful things. If God wanted us girls tottering around like a bunch of drunken sailors, we'd have been

*born wearing stilts! When I was your age, I didn't
particularly care for boys and makeup either. I spent a
lot of time staring at the horizon, wondering what was
just beyond, and when my real life was going to start.
Now that I'm older, I know real life is every day, every
moment, and it's a treasure.*

*And speaking of treasures, I've enclosed this treasure
box charm. Acts of kindness are like jewels: You store
up enough of them in your heart, and you will have
found one of the best treasures of all. For your next
task, I want you to do something nice for someone. Do
it anonymously, without expecting anything in return.
Then you will have earned your charm, and you may
place it on your bracelet. Send me a letter when you're
all through and let me know how it went.*

Just as Violet finished reading, Ms. Zubov brought
out our orders of zucchini fries. Her hands—which were
webbed with thick purple veins—curled unnaturally
around our plates.

"Arthritis," she said, following my stare.

"Does it hurt?" I asked.

"I get by just fine."

After Ms. Zubov left, Violet said, "What act of kindness are you planning to do?"

"I'm not sure yet," I said, taking a bite of a zucchini fry. I'd been thinking about different ideas all day, but so far none of them felt right. "I thought maybe—"

"Hello, Violet!" The Rotary Man with the cap and wire-rimmed glasses stopped at our table. "Are you coming to my shop today? Bob would really like someone to pet him."

Violet nodded and swallowed a fry. "Yeah, just as soon as Izzy and I are finished."

"Izzy?" He turned to me. "You wouldn't happen to be Isabella Malone, Mildred's great-niece, would you?"

"Yes, sir," I said. "Do you know Aunt Mildred?"

"I do indeed. Or I did, at any rate. I haven't seen her since high school. But I heard she was back in town." He stuck out his hand. "My name's Marty McGee."

"Pleased to meet you." I took his outstretched hand and shook it. Then a thought occurred to me. "Are you related to Scooter McGee?"

He laughed. "I see my reputation precedes me. He and I are one and the same! Please tell Mildred I said hello. And tell your mother she has my vote." He tipped his cap and left.

"Who's Bob?" I asked.

"His cat," Violet answered. "He's the fattest one I've ever seen. Mr. McGee owns the Dusty Shelf, the used-book store a few shops over. I go over there after school a lot to look at books and pet Bob."

I figured Violet probably spends a lot of time in Dandelion Square. Her dad owns Barnaby Antiques, a shop on the other side of the village green.

Violet read the letter again while we ate our fries. Then she dug out her glittery purple journal from her backpack and wrote down "Whippie," right after the words "tatter" and "sizzle."

"Is that a list?" I asked.

"Yeah, I keep a list of words I like." She stuffed the journal back in her backpack. "So, what were you thinking about doing to earn your charm?"

"I've got a little bit of allowance money with me." I pulled out a five-dollar bill. "I could give it away anonymously." I opened up a menu, tucked the bill inside, and closed it up again. "There, mission accomplished. Isn't that kind?"

"Very kind." Violet nodded.

We stared at each other until I sighed and said, "But also very boring."

"Exponentially boring," she agreed.

We both munched on our fries while we thought about this. Violet kept wiping up crumbs practically the second they landed on the table. I hadn't remembered her being so neat.

"We could do something else," she said suddenly.

"*We?*"

"Yeah, do you remember how we used to make up secret missions?"

I nodded. When we would pretend to be CIA agents we'd mess around with our walkie-talkies and imagine we were sent to exotic locations to spy on our enemies.

"What if we anonymously cleaned out Ms. Zubov's garden tonight?" Violet said. "You saw her hands. I'll bet it's real difficult for her to keep up her garden. Plus"—she made a face—"I am so sick of eating zucchini. Maybe if we harvest some of her pumpkins she'll finally change her menu. Do you have a cell phone?"

"Not allowed," I said. Mom bought Carolyn a cell phone before she started middle school, but this past summer she told me I couldn't have one because I wasn't "responsible enough."

"What about your walkie-talkie? Do you still have it?"

I nodded. "I think it's in my closet somewhere."

"Okay, find it, and I'll call you on it. Maybe we could meet up around seven thirty. Can you get out tonight?"

Dad worked late at the station on Tuesday nights, and I knew Mom was planning on attending Carolyn's first practice for the school musical, and they wouldn't be home until pretty late. Since Grandma Bertie and Aunt Mildred usually went to bed early, that meant I'd be sitting home alone doing nothing.

"Tonight's good," I said.

We finished eating and then stood up and headed for the door. I left the fiver in the menu. Violet went to visit Bob the cat at the Dusty Shelf, and I nearly skipped as I walked home. Doing something nice for someone with Violet, *and* reviving our secret missions? It was gonna be awesome.

After all, what could go wrong?

CHAPTER 10

SOMETHING GOES WRONG

Tonight's episode of *Izzy Gets In Trouble (Again)* is brought to you by the Hammer, aka Ms. Harmer, Joy-Killer Extraordinaire:

For viewers just tuning in, it began after dinner when Mom called me into the den. She was flipping through a stack of mail while Carolyn was sprawled out on the couch, softly strumming her guitar.

"We have to leave in a few minutes for rehearsal," Mom said. "But I wanted to ask how Mrs. Whippie's charm school is going." She squinted at an envelope then tossed it into the trash.

"It's going fine," I said. "I'm supposed to do something nice for someone anonymously. I put a five-dollar bill in a menu at the Kaleidoscope, but—"

"That was from you?" Carolyn said. "Layla found it when we stopped by earlier. She treated us both to hot chocolates. Thanks!"

"You're welcome," I said. "But I thought that was kind of boring, though, so—"

"Doing something nice for someone is never boring," Mom said.

I was about to tell her all about clearing Ms. Zubov's garden tonight, but right then she held out an envelope from school addressed to *The Parents of Isabella Malone.*

"What's this?" she asked.

"How should I know?" I said, although I had a pretty good idea.

She opened the letter, and sure enough, I was right.

"It's from Ms. Harmer. It says you frequently refuse to follow instructions." She paused and said, "Well?"

I frowned. "Well, what?"

"Well—what do you have to say for yourself?"

"I guess I would say . . . instructions are for kids who have no imagination."

Mom sighed loudly and ran a hand through her hair,

but behind her back Carolyn grinned and gave me a thumbs-up.

"What? You told me to say something, so I did."

Mom read the letter again. "Apparently, you were supposed to write an essay about a famous poet, and instead you turned in a story."

"So what? Ms. Harmer didn't actually say it had to be a *real life* famous poet—so I made one up." If you ask me, what I did was actually harder, and, the best part of all, it only took me fifteen minutes. I wrote a story about a poet named Wanda Wordsmith who went fishing for her poems. Except instead of a fishing pole, she used a kite to catch her words on the wind. I thought it was a great story and deserved an A. But apparently, the Hammer thought it deserved a note home, which made no sense to me at all. Sometimes I think teachers like Ms. Harmer view creativity as something dirty and slightly embarrassing, and would prefer to turn kids into people who color inside the lines.

Generally speaking, I don't care much for lines.

"She shouldn't have had to specify she meant a real poet, Isabella. It was implied."

"My name is *Izzy*. And if Ms. Harmer wanted to learn something about real poets, why couldn't she just Google them herself?"

"The point," Mom said in a steely voice, "was that you were supposed to do research in the library and compile facts, so *you* could learn something."

"I'm allergic to libraries." All that dust and crusty old Mrs. Menzel, the school librarian. *No thanks.* "Besides," I added, "imagination is better than facts."

Mom closed her eyes and took a deep breath. A few of them, actually. "Go upstairs and do your homework. We'll talk about this tomorrow morning when your dad is home."

"Okay, but don't you want to hear about how I'm going to earn my—"

"No, I don't!" Mom's eyes flew open. "I don't want to hear about it. I want you to go upstairs and, for just this once, do what you're told without complaining and arguing!"

"All right, fine! I just thought for once *you* might want to hear about my life!" I stomped up the stairs as loudly as I could, expecting Mom to holler at me to keep it down. She didn't, though, which I guessed made perfect sense.

After all, it's not like she ever listened to me, anyway.

At precisely 7:15, a burst of static escaped from my walkie-talkie, which I'd managed to dig out of my closet.

"Wordnerd to Stargazer, do you copy?"

"This is Stargazer," I said, smiling at our old code names. "I read you, Wordnerd." I quickly turned down the volume. "Report your position."

"I am en route and heading northeast to Dandelion Square. ETA five minutes."

"I'm right behind you, Wordnerd. Over and out."

Quickly, I dumped out the contents of my backpack and stuffed it with the walkie-talkie, a flashlight, Mom's old gardening gloves, my pack of star stickers (I wanted to show them to Violet), and a water bottle. Last, I stuffed my bracelet and the treasure box charm in my pocket. As soon as we finished clearing out the garden I planned to add the charm to my bracelet.

The doors to Grandma Bertie's and Aunt Mildred's rooms were closed, and I held my breath as I tiptoed downstairs, hoping they wouldn't hear me. Mom was usually too distracted to care about my comings and goings, but Grandma Bertie and Aunt Mildred were a lot stricter. I opened the front door and nearly gave a shout when I heard the porch swing creaking and voices murmuring.

"I just miss him so much." Grandma Bertie sniffed, and I knew she was crying again over Grandpa Frank, who died a couple years ago.

"We all miss someone," Aunt Mildred said, and her voice held a strange tone. I couldn't tell if she was mad or sad.

"Oh Milly, I know. I know we do."

I stepped outside and softly closed the door behind me. The porch swing was off to the side of the house, so Grandma Bertie and Aunt Mildred couldn't see me. I could see them, though. They had their arms wrapped around each other, and their white hair rippled in the wind. One of the wooden floorboards squeaked as I inched toward the porch steps.

"Is someone there?" called Aunt Mildred. "Is that you, Izzy?"

I pressed myself into the shadows and held my breath.

"It's probably just the wind, dear," said Grandma Bertie. "Izzy was in her room not ten minutes ago. I swear, you can't remember anything these days, can you?"

"I'll tell you what I remember," Aunt Mildred said, her voice filling with indignation. "I remember . . ."

I made a run for it while the two of them started bickering. The night was dark and clear, the moon was just a small slice of silver, and Orion and Big D were watching me as I made my way up the street. "I'm going to earn my charm," I whispered to them.

I only lived a few streets away from Dandelion Square, so pretty soon I was crouching down behind the slide in the village green's playground. Nearly all of the stores in Dandelion Square were closed. Many of the shops' owners—like Ms. Zubov—lived in apartments above their stores, and most of the second-story windows glowed with buttery yellow light. While I waited for Violet, I pulled out my bag of star stickers. They were glowing in the dark, and they turned my hands a spooky shade of green.

The playground was at the edge of the village green, near a row of street parking, and I drew back farther behind the slide when I heard voices and the clicking of high heels.

"Then you need to try *harder*." It was Mayor Franklin, Stella the Terrible's mother.

"I am," Stella protested. "That was the best I could do."

"Clearly it's not. A B-minus is completely unacceptable." A nearby white SUV made a loud *beep, beep* sound, and Mayor Franklin strode up and pulled open the driver's door. "I won't tolerate it, Stella. Do you understand me? . . . Stella? . . . Are you listening? What are you looking at?"

"Nothing," Stella said.

Both car doors shut, and soon the SUV was pulling away. I couldn't believe Mayor Franklin was so upset over a B-minus. If I got a B-minus, Mom would probably die of shock.

Wondering what was taking Violet so long, I put my stickers away and pulled out my walkie-talkie. "Stargazer to Wordnerd," I whispered. "Do you copy?"

"I'm right behind you," Violet said, and dropped down next to me.

"Where have you been?"

"Casing the joint. The Kaleidoscope is closed, and I think Ms. Zubov is watching TV upstairs." She pointed at the window above the café, which flickered with blue light. "The area is pretty much deserted. I think we could go around the side of the café to the back without a problem." She stood up. "Ready?"

"Ready," I said, also standing. I imagined how pleased Ms. Zubov would be when she came out to her garden tomorrow and saw all the work we'd done.

"Good. Operation Earn Your Charm is a go."

When we reached the backyard, it looked like Violet was right, and Ms. Zubov was having a hard time keeping up with her garden. Weeds wound themselves around the squash plants, and the tomato vines were limp and brown and needed to be ripped out completely. She also had a patch bursting with pumpkins that needed harvesting.

"This is one huge garden," Violet said.

"Yeah, I guess we'd better get to it." I yanked on a large weed and felt a satisfying *whoosh* as the root unearthed. The plants were slightly spiky and scratched at my hands. I unzipped my backpack and put on Mom's gardening gloves.

Violet and I worked silently by the glow of our flashlights. I wanted to slide back into friendship with her the way you can always slide back into your favorite pair of jeans. Except I forgot that sometimes when you finally get around to washing those jeans they shift and shrink and don't fit quite as well anymore. That's how it felt with me and Violet: stiff and a little uncomfortable.

The wind picked up, and the back of my neck began to prickle. I turned around to look at the café.

Someone was standing on the back porch, watching us.

I swallowed a scream—then stopped short when I realized there wasn't anyone there. Not a real, live person, anyway. It was a large cutout of my mother, emblazoned with the slogan JANINE MALONE, JUST WHAT DANDELION HOLLOW NEEDS! at the bottom. I had forgotten all about the campaign materials being dropped off at the café.

I wandered over to the porch and shined my flashlight on the cutout. It was supposed to be life-size, but while Mom was only five one, the cutout was a good six feet tall. Next to it was a large cardboard box. I figured it was the new campaign mailers with our family photo.

All week I had been dreading seeing the dorky photo of my family. I figured as soon as all the kids at school saw, it would give them one more reason to tease me.

I opened the box. Mom and Dad and Carolyn grinned at the camera. Carolyn was in the middle, holding her guitar. A not-so-subtle reminder, I was sure, that their daughter was Carolyn the Great, Dandelion Hollow's only bona fide prodigy.

It looked great. Except it was one daughter short.

Mom's new campaign mailer, the one advertising her perfect family, the one that was going out to every house in town, didn't have me in it.

It felt like a herd of angry elephants was stampeding across my heart. I knew I didn't have Carolyn's talent, or her mild manners. I knew whatever hopes Mom had for me—if she had any at all—didn't include a scholarship to a fancy school or a lifetime full of amazing achievements. And most days, I was okay with that. I loved Carolyn too, and I wanted her to go out and conquer the world, one song at a time.

But looking at that photograph, it felt like I'd been erased from my own family.

"Izzy, can you help me?" Violet called. "Ms. Zubov has some baskets by her toolshed. I'm going to fill them with pumpkins."

"Be there in a second," I said.

I couldn't tear my eyes away from the photo. I knew Mom didn't understand me. Truthfully, I didn't understand her either. But was I really so much of an embarrassment that she thought it was better not to include me at all?

The breeze picked up; Ms. Zubov's wind chimes started clanging, and a few of the mailers blew straight out of the box and into the garden. I should have closed the box right then, but I didn't. I kept staring at the cutout, at Mom's smiling face, and my hands, which often don't listen to my brain, started taking orders from my heart.

I pushed the cutout. Not too hard, but hard enough that the wind took over. The cutout toppled over the porch and landed in a mud puddle with a loud *thud*.

"What are you *doing*?" Violet asked.

I couldn't answer her. I just stared at the muddy cut-out, while the wind carried away more mailers in a snow-storm of paper.

The porch lights clicked on and the back door cracked open an inch. "Who's there?" Ms. Zubov yelled. "You should know I've got a Taser and I'm not afraid to use it!"

"It's just us—" Violet began, but her voice was drowned out by the wind chimes and Ms. Zubov hollering, "I mean it! If I have to come back there I will fry you like an egg!" There was a *pop*, a *hiss*, and the metallic smell of an electrical current.

Panic filled Violet's eyes, and she took off running. I hesitated for a second, then grabbed my backpack and started after her. We ran all the way back to our neighborhood, autumn leaves blowing away as our feet pounded the pavement. We stopped under a lamppost and tried to catch our breath.

"She would've done it," Violet gasped. "She would've tased us."

"Yep," I said, panting, "our brains would be as good as scrambled—maybe she'd even add them to tomorrow's menu."

We looked at each other, and then suddenly, we were laughing. Real, honest-to-goodness, tears-down-your-cheeks, can't-catch-your-breath laughter. It felt good. I couldn't remember the last time I'd laughed like that.

"It looks like you earned your charm," Violet said, straightening up.

"I guess I did." I took my bracelet and the charm out of my pocket. Carefully, I hooked the tiny treasure box onto the gold chain, then slipped the bracelet over my wrist. Just then, the lamplight flickered. The treasure box sparkled in the light, and the bracelet seemed to glow. It didn't make me feel completely better about Mom's mailer. But it helped a little.

"It really is pretty," Violet said, staring at my bracelet. She frowned. "When you write to Mrs. Whippie, tell her she should send *me* a bracelet and a charm, too. I'm pretty sure I earned it tonight."

11

SORE THUMBS AND
PRETTY PINKIES

Dear Mrs. Whippie,

I did your anonymous act of kindness, like you asked. I hope you don't mind, but a girl named Violet and I turned it into a secret mission. I had a lot of fun, for the first time in a long while. Well, up until I found out that my mom thinks I'm an embarrassment to the family. But I guess that's why she signed me up for your school in the first place.

My mom and I got into a fight today. Truthfully, we get into fights most days, possibly because I haven't learned what my sister, Carolyn, calls the Subtle Art of Shutting Up.

Carolyn is a musical genius, and sometimes that's kind of hard for me. It wouldn't be so bad if she were a horrible person and a mean sister, but she's actually a very lovely person and a pretty spectacular sister. And to make things even worse, she gets good grades. I'm pretty sure my mom wishes I was more like her.

I don't know if you know this, but the streets in Dandelion Hollow are named after wildflowers. Sometimes I feel like a wildflower. Not particularly refined, and always popping up where I'm not supposed to. Except wildflowers are beautiful, and most of the time I feel like a sore thumb in a room full of pretty pinkies.

Anyways, I like my bracelet, but I think it will look even prettier when there are more charms on it. Which reminds me, do you think you could send me a bracelet and a treasure box charm for Violet? I think she wants to join your school too.

Your Friend,
Izzy Malone

CHAPTER
12

A TRAIL OF STARS

The next morning, after I placed Mrs. Whippie's letter in the mailbox, I headed for the kitchen. Breakfast is a big deal in my house. Mom usually handles dinner, but Aunt Mildred and Grandma Bertie are in charge of breakfast, and they take it pretty seriously. No one is ever allowed out of the house without a full plate of eggs, sausage, and whatever else the two of them decide to cook up.

Mom was staring glumly out the window when I sat down at the table. Grandma Bertie and Aunt Mildred were fussing over her: refilling her coffee, grating Parmesan cheese onto her avocado omelet, and buttering her toast on both sides, just the way she likes it.

"You need to eat something," Grandma Bertie said, squeezing Mom's shoulder.

"Not hungry," Mom answered.

I wondered if maybe she was coming down with a cold, and I started to ask if she was okay, but then I remembered the mailers from last night.

Carolyn came stumbling into the kitchen, bleary-eyed and pale, her hair sticking up every which way. "Morning." After she sat down, she rested her head on the table. She looked so different from the glowing picture on Mom's mailer—the one I apparently wasn't allowed to be in.

"Wow," I said. "You look really terrible."

"Thanks a lot—I had a ton of homework last night after we got home. I wish practice hadn't run so late."

"I think your face wishes the same thing."

Carolyn looked up. "What is your problem?"

"Nothing," I said. "It just must be real exhausting, being such an in-demand star."

"Izzy, dear, your mouth is acting up again." Grandma Bertie slid hot mugs topped with whipped cream in front of me and Carolyn.

"What's this?" I asked.

"Cinnamon hot chocolate. Guaranteed to cure tiredness—and bad attitudes."

"Sorry," I mumbled. Most of the time, I remembered it wasn't Carolyn's fault Mom was the way she was, but some days were harder than others, and today was definitely one of them.

"No problem at all." Carolyn sipped her mug and smiled back at me with a whipped cream mustache. "Dork."

"Loser." I stuck out my tongue.

"Girls!" Aunt Mildred snapped as she passed around more plates of omelets. "Let's try acting our age this morning."

"Oh, yeah?" I said. "What's *your* age, Aunt Mildred?"

Carolyn snickered as she poked reluctantly at her omelet. "Most of my friends just eat donuts for breakfast," she said.

"And you wonder why all you young people are so tired all the time," Aunt Mildred said. "All that sugar. It's a disgrace. It's—"

"It's nearly six thirty, that's what it is," Dad said, striding into the kitchen, dressed in his uniform. "I need to get to the station early."

"Not before you've eaten, you don't." Grandma Bertie handed him a cup of coffee.

Dad grimaced and sat down. It was pretty hard to say

no to the combined forces of Grandma Bertie and Aunt Mildred, especially when they were getting along and armed with steaming mugs of early morning sustenance.

Dad chugged his coffee and forked a big bite of omelet into his mouth. "Got to get moving," he mumbled. "Got a new case to work on."

"In Dandelion Hollow?" Carolyn asked skeptically. "What's happened?"

Dad shot Mom a strange look; Mom ignored it, and concentrated on her coffee while Grandma Bertie gave her shoulder another squeeze.

"Last night we got a call from Ms. Zubov," Dad said. "Apparently, she heard vandals poking around her back-yard last night."

Vandals? I felt like the eggs I'd just swallowed were about to come back up. *No, it couldn't be*, I thought.

But it was.

"It was the strangest thing, though," Dad continued. "It looks like the vandals actually cleaned up her garden."

"That doesn't sound like vandalism to me," Carolyn said.

"It is if they damage someone else's property." Dad paused, and glanced over at Mom, who avoided his gaze. "Your mother had her new campaign materials delivered to Ms. Zubov's to keep for the time being. The vandals destroyed it all last night."

The table went quiet, but my heart thundered in my ears. This could *not* be happening.

"They destroyed it?" Carolyn repeated, looking shocked. She turned to Mom. "Are you okay?"

"Of course I'm okay," Mom said in a monotone, still concentrating on her coffee. "Someone hates me enough to try and sabotage my campaign. Why wouldn't I be okay?"

"Sabotage?" Grandma Bertie's hand fluttered to her mouth. "I hadn't thought of it that way. Can you imagine? Campaign sabotage in Dandelion Hollow? Wait till the Knatterers hear about this."

Grandma Bertie was part of a knitting circle that was known just as much for their gossiping as they were for their stitching. Everyone in town called them the Knattering Knitters.

"That is just plain speculation, Bertha," Aunt Mildred said. "You don't know that for sure, so don't go running that mouth of yours all over town."

"It's my mouth, Mildred, and I'll run it as much as I like. And speaking of big mouths—"

"What if it was an accident?" I asked. "What if they didn't mean to damage Mom's stuff?"

"That's unlikely," Dad answered in between bites of his omelet. "He ruined a cutout of your mother and tossed her new mailers all over the back of Ms. Zubov's garden. Although why he bothered to clean up the garden in the first place, I don't know."

"He?" Carolyn said. "Do you have any suspects?"

Dad shook his head. "Not really. But Ms. Zubov said there were some ornery high school boys in the café yesterday."

I looked down at my omelet and pushed my plate away before I puked. I'd been so upset about the photo last night, I hadn't thought how Ms. Zubov's backyard would look to other people. I hadn't closed the box of mailers, and with the wind, I'm sure the rest of them blew straight into her yard after Violet and I ran away.

"But we do have one lead," Dad said. "A trail of star stickers littered Ms. Zubov's garden, from the porch all the way back to Thistle Road. I stopped by last night after she called the station, and it made a neon trail—it was like the vandals *wanted* us to know they'd been there."

My hand flew down to my backpack, where my packet of star stickers was still stashed. Violet and I had started running so fast—had the stickers spilled out then? I leaned down to check and, sure enough, the pack was now only a quarter full. But there were still enough left that the inside of my backpack held a soft glow. *Great job, Izzy, leaving evidence at the scene of the crime.*

Except I hadn't committed a crime. Not intentionally, anyway. I'd been trying to help Ms. Zubov, not hurt Mom.

"Izzy, what are you doing?" Aunt Mildred asked.

Hastily, I zipped up my backpack. "I was just checking on a homework assignment."

Was it my imagination, or did Aunt Mildred stare at me just a little too long while she sipped her coffee?

"Ms. Zubov said you and Violet Barnaby were in the café yesterday," Dad said. "Did you see anything unusual?"

"I saw . . ." For a moment, I was tempted to tell him everything. But then I thought of all the trouble I'd been getting in, and the way Mom looked at me sometimes. Would they really believe it was an accident, or would they think I was truly turning into a juvenile delinquent?

"What did you see, Izzy?" Grandma Bertie was leaning so far over the table her sleeves dipped into her omelet.

"I saw . . . I saw Scooter McGee," I finished.

"Scooter McGee." Grandma Bertie batted her eyes at Aunt Mildred. "However is he?"

"He seemed good. He asked about you, Aunt Mildred."

Grandma Bertie pounded her fist on the table. "I *told*

you he was still sweet on you, Milly! I see a whirlwind romance in your future."

"And I see a black eye in yours, Bertha, if you don't shut it."

As Grandma Bertie and Aunt Mildred began to argue, I excused myself from the table, saying I needed to finish getting ready for the day. A little while later, I still felt bad for Mom, so I decided to give her the pot full of sunflowers I'd picked a week ago. The door to her bedroom was slightly ajar, and I saw Mom standing in front of her dresser. She was having a conversation with her mirror: "You are powerful, Janine. You are strong, and people want to be your friend." She paused, then started up again. "You are powerful, Janine . . ."

There was something sad and embarrassing about watching Mom chant over and over again to her pained reflection, and I knew she'd be angry if she realized I'd seen.

I placed the pot of sunflowers on the hallway table and left, feeling about as low as an earthworm.

CHAPTER
13

LEFTOVERS

A middle school cafeteria can be the loneliest place in the world if you care to eat there, which I definitely do not. But since I didn't eat breakfast, and I'd forgotten my lunch at home, I took my place in the cafeteria line and hoped that whatever was being served today would vaguely resemble actual food.

I'd looked all over school for Violet so I could tell her about our new careers as campaign-sabotaging vandals, but so far I hadn't seen her.

The line slowly inched forward. Lauren Wilcox and some of the other Paddlers were a few places in front of me. I couldn't hear what they were talking about, so I moved in a little closer.

"Excuse me," said the girl in front of me. "Would you mind not standing so close?" I muttered a "sorry" and stepped back.

I paid for my lunch and my stomach wound itself into knots as I held my tray and looked around, trying to decide where to sit and feeling like a leftover piece of pizza that no one wants. Maybe I was waiting for someone to come up and say, *Hi, Izzy. Want to sit with me?* But of course no one did.

Austin was sitting with Tyler Jones and Trent Walker at a nearby table. "Ribbit, ribbit!" Tyler said when he saw me staring. Austin elbowed him, and Tyler shut right up, but Austin wouldn't look at me. We hadn't played basketball since our fight, and I wondered if that was just how it was going to be from now on. Mom had tried to give me a speech over the summer about how boys and girls don't always stay friends after elementary school ends, but the minute she said the word "puberty," I stuck my fingers in my ears and started singing.

Sophia Ramos, a girl from my history class, was sitting by herself at a table, and I could swear she half waved at

me as I passed by. I considered turning around and joining
her, but I decided not to because:

    a. I wasn't completely sure she'd actually
       been waving at me, and not someone
       behind me.

    b. Even if she was waving at me, Sophia
       had just moved to Dandelion Hollow
       right before school started, and she
       probably didn't know that sitting with
       me could mean three solid years of
       being a potential middle school outcast,
       and I didn't think that was fair to her.
       And most important . . .

    c. Right then I spied an empty table behind
       the Paddlers, which would give me an
       excellent opportunity to listen to them.

"Everyone needs to be there at four this afternoon,"
Lauren was saying as I sat down.

Where at four? I leaned back, closer to the Paddlers.

"Hey, Toad Girl," Stella called. "Eavesdrop much?"

The Paddlers laughed, and Stella made the *ribbit, ribbit*
sound that had chased me around the last couple years.

The bell rang, and the Paddlers began clearing their trays, and Lauren called out, "Don't forget: four o'clock, Caulfield Farm. Be there."

Instantly, I felt better, for the first time all day. I knew where the Paddlers were going after school, and when they were gonna be there. Life was suddenly looking up.

CHAPTER 14

CAULFIELD FARM

"You know," Mom said, as she started the car, "when you go to a meeting like this, it's important to put your best foot forward."

I had no idea what she was talking about, but I looked down at my combat-booted feet and wondered which one was better. "Well," I said slowly, "I'm right-handed, so maybe—"

"No, it's just an expression," Mom said, irritation creeping into her voice. "It means to try and make a good impression. To show people your best side."

"Oh, okay." I paused. "What's the best side of me?"

Mom's hands tightened up on the steering wheel. "Oh

well, there's *lots* of great things about you. You're a nice girl, for one thing, and you're really very . . . spirited. And, well . . ." She fumbled about some more before lapsing into silence, but I knew the truth: Most parents like to brag about their kid's grades or other accomplishments. But I never got on the honor roll, and I wasn't a musical prodigy like Carolyn. The only thing I seemed to be good at was getting into trouble.

Mom turned the car down the long gravel road leading to Caulfield Farm, and I stared silently out the window. As soon as I heard Lauren mention the farm I knew she'd been talking about the volunteer meeting for Pumpkin Palooza this afternoon, because Mom was going to it too. It wasn't too difficult to convince Mom to let me tag along, but now I was having second thoughts. Mom was obviously annoyed, and she was gripping the steering wheel so tightly her knuckles were white.

"Is everything okay?" I asked, then immediately wished I hadn't, because I was sure she was still upset about her campaign materials getting damaged.

Which is all your fault, I reminded myself.

"I'm fine," Mom answered. "I'm just dreading the meeting, I guess. Everyone knows what happened last night—I already received a bunch of phone calls this morning."

Figures. In Dandelion Hollow, everyone knows every-one else's business. Grandma Bertie says it's one of the great things about living in a small town. Aunt Mildred says it's the reason she packed her bags and left the minute she turned eighteen.

"I just can't believe somebody would deliberately sab-otage my campaign," Mom said in a soft voice. "I've never heard of such a thing in Dandelion Hollow."

I didn't know what to say; it wasn't often that Mom talked to me about things that really mattered, and I felt worse than ever. I considered coming clean again, but I couldn't bring myself to do it. We were already on shaky ground—things would totally explode if she knew I was responsible for messing up her campaign stuff.

We drove the rest of the way in silence, and soon Caulfield Farm came into view. It was the biggest farm in Dandelion Hollow, and one of my favorite places in town. I loved everything about it: the big pumpkin patch, the Caulfields' big farmhouse, the red barn, the fir lot where everyone in town buys their Christmas trees, and Caulfield Pond, which is either a huge pond or a small lake, depend-ing on who you ask. Now that it was October, all the maple leaves were aflame with color, and I could already taste the apple cider the Caulfields brewed in the fall.

Mom parked the car and shut the engine off, but we didn't get out right away. First, she had to brush her hair and fix her makeup. After all, Candidate Malone could not be seen in public looking anything less than perfect.

While I waited, I rolled down the window and made faces at myself in the side mirror.

"Knock it off," Mom said. "What will people think?"

"I don't care what people think," I said, making another face. I was trying to mimic the way Ms. Harmer looks when a kid doesn't turn in their homework assignment: sort of constipated, and sort of like she has fire ants crawling on her insides, all at the same time. I was pretty sure Austin would think my impression was dead-on, and I was looking forward to showing him if we started speaking again.

"You really don't care, do you?" When I looked back at Mom she was staring at me, an unreadable expression on her face.

"No," I said. "I don't."

We stared at each other, until Mom sighed and stuck her lipstick back in her purse. "Let's go," she said.

The farm was owned by an elderly couple—everyone called them Grandpa and Grandma Caulfield—and when we stepped inside the farmhouse they both greeted us warmly.

"Janine Malone, we are certainly glad to see you today," Grandpa Caulfield said, pulling Mom into a hug.

"That's right," Grandma Caulfield said in her no-non-sense voice. "We heard about what happened last night. Hold your head high, girl, and smile. Don't let the nitwits in town get you down."

"Thanks, Grandma Caulfield," Mom said, and she actually did smile then.

"Everyone's gathering in the kitchen," Grandpa Caulfield said. "We'll start the meeting in a few minutes."

Mom and I followed the spicy scent of hot cider down the hall. The kitchen was large and decorated with plaid wallpaper. Several volunteers crowded around a big wooden island where Stella the Terrible was opening up Tupperware containers full of homemade cookies. They were frosted with a big "MF." For "Mayor Franklin." You know, just to make sure everyone knew exactly who we had to thank for the afternoon's culinary confections. The rest of the Paddlers were passing them around to everyone.

"Thanks," I said brightly to Lauren when she handed me a plate. "The cookies look . . . ," I began, but she barely glanced at me before walking away.

"*We* should have thought of this," Mom hissed, staring at her plate furiously. "People like free food."

Personally, I didn't think a few cookies were going to cost Mom the election, but I figured putting my best foot forward meant keeping my big mouth shut, so I kept quiet.

Monogrammed or not, the cookies looked good. They smelled good too. I picked one up and bit into it. Snickerdoodles—my favorite. I was finishing my third one when Mayor Franklin came over to give Mom her signature greeting: a side hug followed by a couple air kisses, which I happen to know Mom thinks is over-the-top and pretentious, but you'd never know it by the smile she pasted on her face.

"Janine, it's so nice to see you," Mayor Franklin said. She stepped closer to me, and I got a whiff of her perfume, which was so sickly sweet it rammed itself up your nose and down your throat and made you want to puke your ever-lovin' guts out.

"I'm happy to be here," Mom said.

"Under the circumstances, no one would've faulted you for skipping the meeting." She shook her head. "Sabotage just cannot be tolerated."

"I'm not entirely sure it was sabotage," Mom said, her smile stretching tight. "It could have just been an accident."

Mayor Franklin threw back her head and laughed. "Oh

Janine, be serious! *Of course* it was sabotage. But I want you to know, just because someone out there really, *really* doesn't want you to be mayor doesn't mean I don't think you can give my campaign a good run for its money!"

"Thank you," Mom said archly. "I'll keep that in mind."

Mayor Franklin laughed again and turned to me. "Izzy, it's nice to see you, too," she said, which was a big fat lie, judging by the way her smile wilted. "I was sorry to hear you didn't make the Paddlers, like Stella."

"Actually, I beat Stella at tryouts by three-tenths of a second."

"You did not!" Stella said, coming up behind me.

"Isabella," Mom warned. "Stop."

"Izzy. And stop *what*? Mrs. Franklin was at tryouts; she already knows." Mayor Franklin, unlike my own mom, who was too busy to come to the aquatic center, had spent both days of tryouts chatting with Lauren Wilcox's mom. Big wonder why they picked Stella over me.

"Isabella," Mom said again, her face turning red, "you're being impolite."

I crammed a cookie into my mouth before it could decide to say anything else. I could never figure out why adults said you were being impolite, when all you were doing was telling the truth. Maybe "being polite" in this situation meant pretending none of us could read a stop-watch.

Mom wrapped an arm around me and gave me a squeeze. A hard one. "Isabella's going to be volunteering in my booth during Pumpkin Palooza."

"I am?" Both Mom and Mrs. Franklin had been given a booth where they could set up their campaign materials, but I had planned on spending all morning getting ready for the regatta.

"Yes. Don't you remember?" Mom shot me her be-quiet-or-you-will-die-young look.

"Right, I forgot."

Mrs. Franklin's smile was nowhere to be found. "Are you sure that's a good idea, Janine? I mean, she's your daughter, and I'm sure you know what's best, it's just, I've heard some troubling things about Izzy lately. For instance, I heard how she started a food fight in the cafeteria on the first day of school."

"*Attempted* to start a food fight," Stella said, smirking. "No one would join her."

I didn't *attempt* to do anything, except sit with Paddlers. I figured maybe if they got to know me then the next time a spot opened up on the team they'd pick me. But a few minutes after I sat down, a girl with glittery eye shadow said, "Aren't you Carolyn Malone's little sister? I heard her sing once—she's really talented." She cocked her head. "It's too bad you're not more like her." Of course, nobody cares about *that*. All anyone cares about is that Glitter Girl concluded lunchtime plastered in my portion of mashed potatoes.

And I made my first trip to Coco Martin's office, a mere four hours after starting the school year.

I'm told it was a new school record. Applaud if you must.

"We'll both be fine, Kendra," Mom said. "But thank you for your concern. Now, about Pumpkin Palooza . . ."

I didn't want to hear any more, so I walked over to the kitchen table. Daisy Caulfield, Grandpa and Grandma Caulfield's actual granddaughter, was ladling cider into mugs, a sour look on her face. Her hair was cut short in a blond bob, and she was wearing the same brown leather jacket she always wore.

I didn't know too much about Daisy. She moved back to Dandelion Hollow a couple years ago with her mom, and she was homeschooled up until last month. We had the same math class, but she pretty much kept to herself.

"I don't have time to be doing this," Daisy grumbled

as I took a mug of cider. "I have an assignment I need to be working on."

I didn't know what to say to that. I'd ladle a thousand mugs before I'd willingly do homework. A million, probably. But at least she wasn't calling me Toad Girl.

"Yeah, Mr. Snyder assigned a lot of algebra problems today, didn't he?" I said, although I couldn't be too sure, because I'd sort of accidentally-on-purpose left my textbook in my locker.

"Are you kidding? I wasn't talking about *homework*." She paused, and added, "Actually, it's something you could help me with. I really need to talk to you—"

"All right, everyone, gather around." At the back of the kitchen, a girl wearing bell bottoms and pink tinted glasses waved her hands.

"Who is *that*?" Mom said, coming up next to me. "Why are the Caulfields letting a teenager run the meeting?"

I shook my head, wondering what Daisy had been about to say. No one at school ever really needed to talk to me about anything.

"That's not a teenager; that's Delia," Daisy said. "My mother," she added.

Mom turned bright red. "Oh. Well, I didn't recognize her."

Daisy looked furious, but I don't think it was Mom she was mad at. "That's because *Delia's* going through a phase right now. It's her newest thing."

"I think she looks awesome," I said. "I wonder where she gets her clothes."

"Thank you so much for coming tonight," Delia said, once everyone quieted down. "I know my parents and I are so grateful. As you know, in order to make Pumpkin Palooza successful, we need people to man the games and vendors to serve food." She produced a clipboard. "Please sign up where you'd like to volunteer."

When the clipboard finally came around to Mom and me—after I'd eaten three more cookies—no one had written down their name to help out with Candidate Malone's booth. Stella and the Paddlers had volunteered to help out with Mayor Franklin's booth, though, so all her slots were filled. It made me wish I had a lot of friends, so I could write their names down. I wrote my name in really big letters to try and make up for it.

After the clipboard finished making the rounds, Delia gave some more announcements, then dismissed everyone. Stella, Lauren, and the rest of the Paddlers stood up and left. I knew Mom would spend the next hour or so shaking hands and chatting with everyone, so I decided to follow them.

They headed out of the farmhouse and over to the pond.

By the time I caught up with them, Lauren was pacing back and forth by the Caulfields' canoe. The other girls were lined up in front of her. I crept forward and crouched down behind a nearby bush.

"You all need to be working harder," Lauren was saying. "My mom said everyone at practice was so slow last week that we might as well have stayed home." She turned on Stella. "And *you* were the slowest. You need to pick up your pace if you expect to compete with us. Do you think you can do that?"

"*I* can do that!" I popped up from behind the bush and joined them. "I can row even faster than I did at tryouts. Just watch!"

Everyone jumped. Stella shot daggers at me with her eyes, and Glitter Girl looked like I was a bug she wanted to squash. But I didn't care. Grandma Bertie says life sometimes hands you unexpected opportunities, and you've just got to take them.

I jumped into the canoe and starting paddling. Icy drops hit my face as I plunged the oars into the water over and over, and I reminded myself to be careful and precise. "Your strokes must be quick and elegant," Lauren's mom had said at tryouts.

"Elegant" wasn't a word that would ever describe me, but I could be as quick as a jackrabbit when I wanted. In no time at all, I was heading toward the center of the pond. Crisp air filled my lungs, and I felt my chest lighten. Right then, nothing in the world mattered except the sky above me, the water beneath me, and the fierce beating of my own heart.

I kept going, paddling faster and faster . . . only it seemed like I was slowing down, not speeding up. What the heck?

There was a sharp yank, and the canoe pulled backward.

"Hey, Toad Girl! Next time you want to go for a ride, try untying the boat first!" Stella held up the rope line and gave it another yank, dragging me back a couple inches. Everyone laughed; the Paddlers' ponytails all bobbed in unison.

By the time I rowed myself back to shore, they were long gone.

CHAPTER
15

THE STAR
BANDIT

I had just stepped out of the canoe and was about to head back to the farmhouse when I heard someone behind me cough and say, "Hey."

I turned around. Violet emerged from between two bushes. We stared at each other, and from the look on her face I could tell she'd seen everything.

"So . . . are you volunteering for Pumpkin Palooza?" I asked.

She nodded. "We were running late today, but Dad volunteers every year."

She glanced over in the direction where Lauren and the others had gone and said, "It's sort of embarrassing, the way you hover around them all the time."

"I don't hover," I answered. *Do I hover?* "I barely even talk to them," I added.

"But it's clear you want to. And I heard Lauren telling her friends you hang around her locker, spying on her. I'm just saying," she went on, when I opened my mouth to argue, "you're kind of obvious around them, and I think you're the only one who doesn't see it."

That was something else I had forgotten about Violet: She told you God's honest truth, even if you didn't much want to hear it.

"Why do you even want to be friends with them?" she asked. "They're awful."

I shrugged and looked back at the pond. I didn't know how to tell her that it was about a lot more than just racing. It was about being part of a team and knowing there was a seat saved for you in the cafeteria. It was about knowing you had friends who always had your back, who would call you up if you stayed home from school and ask, *Are you okay?*

It had been a long time since anybody had asked me if I was okay. And sometimes it felt like if I stopped coming to school altogether, no one would notice.

"Izzy," Daisy Caulfield said, coming up behind Violet, "can I talk to you? I was wondering if I could get a quote from your dad for an article I'm writing." She glanced between Violet and me and said, "Is this a bad time?"

"Not really," Violet said.

"Why do you need a quote from my dad?" I asked.

"I write for the *Grapevine*—the school newspaper—and I'm working on a story." Daisy handed me a notepad. Violet read over my shoulder:

The Star Bandit

This week Dandelion Hollow had more excitement than it's seen in a long time, not since Stewart and Ethan Franklin, the sons of our own Mayor Franklin, decided to test an urban myth—and the limits of their own intelligence—by filling the fountain in Dandelion Square with soda and Pop Rocks. On Tuesday night, Ms. Zubov, the owner of the Kaleidoscope Café, Dandelion Hollow's premier eating establishment, happened upon vandals in her backyard. According to Ms. Zubov, she first heard the disturbance around 9:05 p.m.: "I came running outside in my bathrobe armed with nothing but my wits and my own two fists to protect me, and that coward couldn't stand up to an old woman. I'm certain I saw a dim shape fleeing my yard, but by the time I got to Thistle Street, he was gone."

More perplexing than the vandal's apparent cowardice is what he left behind. While it seems he went to great lengths to clean up Ms. Zubov's overgrown garden, he also appears to have damaged campaign materials belonging to mayoral candidate Janine Malone.

Mrs. Malone, a beloved member of our community, was, in her own words, utterly shocked: "I would sincerely hope that good taste and good manners would prevail—no matter how much some people in this community like Mayor Franklin."

Mayor Franklin bristled at the implication that her campaign or its supporters were somehow involved in the incident. "I've known Janine Malone since middle school," Mayor Franklin is quoted as saying. "Believe me; she's capable of losing this election all on her own. Of course," she was quick to add, "I hope these cretins are caught soon."

The cretins in question left behind a calling card of sorts: a trail of star stickers leading off into the night. Sources say this may be the sign of a compulsive criminal, and that the vandal—who some are calling the Star Bandit—may strike again. Of course, the fact that the Star Bandit apparently cleaned up Ms. Zubov's garden has many shaking their heads in confusion. And, thanks to the Star Bandit's efforts, Ms. Zubov wants everyone to know that the Kaleidoscope will now be serving pumpkin muffins, pumpkin pie, and pumpkin cheesecake for the remainder of the month.

So what say you, Grapeviners? Is the Star Bandit a daring do-gooder, or a vicious vandal?

"Vandal?" Violet said when we finished reading. "She thinks a *vandal* was in her garden last night?" She looked at me with wide eyes.

"I heard about it earlier," I said carefully, with a quick glance at Daisy, "but I didn't get the chance to tell you."

"Isn't it great?" Daisy said. "This is the juiciest story to hit Dandelion Hollow in a long time!"

"Who's calling the vandal 'The Star Bandit'?" Violet asked, looking again at the article.

"No one," Daisy admitted. "I made the name up. But it has a nice ring, don't you think?"

"Maybe," I said, "but you got some of the details wrong. Ms. Zubov had a Taser. She didn't come outside to fight anybody off with her fists."

Excuse me, but if someone is going to write an article about me, they could at least get their facts right, and not call me a coward.

Violet elbowed me in the ribs, and Daisy narrowed her eyes. "How do you know that?" she asked.

"Oh," I said quickly, "my dad told me at breakfast this morning."

"Yeah," Violet said. "So why are you lying about it?"

"I'm not lying. It just sounds better my way," Daisy said. "Besides, it's just the school newspaper. Hardly anyone is going to read it, anyway."

CHAPTER 16
CREATIVE JOURNALISM

Daisy was wrong. *Everyone* read her article in the *Grapevine*. It was so popular the *Dandelion Gazette*, the town newspaper, reprinted it (except they took out the part about the Franklin brothers).

"I never said I thought anyone connected to Mayor Franklin was responsible," Mom grumbled at breakfast the day after the article came out.

"Then what did you say, dear?" Grandma Bertie asked.

Judging by the fact that Mom wouldn't answer, what she actually said was probably close enough that I didn't think Daisy was taking too many liberties with her words. Ms. Zubov became an instant town celebrity, and she didn't bother to correct Daisy's account. Dad (who refused to give Daisy a quote) pretended to be annoyed over the idea that the Star Bandit was going to be a repeat offender. But I think he was secretly thrilled to have a real bona fide troublemaker to catch, and was just waiting to see if the Star Bandit would strike again.

Everyone was.

Some girls in my science class were convinced it was a cute boy they'd seen eating at the Kaleidoscope a week ago. Grandma Bertie thought it was an ex-con who she'd heard had escaped from prison last month.

"Why does everyone assume the Star Bandit is a boy?" I complained one afternoon to Austin. He and I still weren't talking, but he had come over with his dad to check on Bozo. Mr. Jackson and Dad were close friends, and Mr. Jackson was going to help Dad get Bozo ready on the day of the regatta. Austin and I were sort of hanging out while they chatted about pollination strategies. I hoped this could be the beginning of a truce between us.

"The Star Bandit has to be a boy," Austin said. "It couldn't be a girl, could it?"

"Do you want me to punch you again? A girl is just as capable of being the Star Bandit."

"Geez, Izzy, I just meant a girl wouldn't have been stupid enough to leave so much evidence behind."

"Stupid?" I put my hands on my hips. "Who are you calling stupid?"

"The Star Bandit, that's who!" After that, Austin stomped back to his house.

So much for a truce.

Meanwhile, Mrs. Whippie's third letter arrived. Mom wordlessly handed it to me while she sorted the mail and talked on the phone to one of the book club ladies. It was sort of hurtful how she never asked about the charm school. Hurtful but not surprising. I guess she figured since I'd gone a whole two weeks without getting in trouble at school, her work was done.

If she only knew.

Violet and I avoided each other; we were both afraid someone would figure out the two of us together were actually the Star Bandit. But the day after Mrs. Whippie's third letter arrived, I tracked Violet down in front of her new English class and asked her to come to my house after school.

"It's about Operation Earn Your Charm," I whispered. "I have something for you," I added.

Violet glanced around and nodded. "I'll be there."

As soon as Violet arrived, we went to my treehouse, where no one would disturb us.

"Nice," Violet said, when she saw the star stickers I'd stuck on the walls. "You'd better hope neither of your parents comes up here, though."

"They won't—I'm the only one who uses it."

After we settled on the floor, I pulled out a photo box where I stored a few small treasures: some leaves I hadn't yet pasted into my journal, a rock I'd found at Dandelion Lake, a miniature trolley car Dad bought me on our last trip to San Francisco. I kept Mrs. Whippie's letters there. I took out her newest and turned it upside down and shook it. Along with the letter, out fell a bracelet, treasure box charm, and two charms each of a palette of paint and a jukebox. The jukebox charms were brown-and-brass-colored and bits of them were painted purple, red, and aqua. The paint palette charms were gold with tiny colored rhinestones for different paint colors.

"These are for you." I handed Violet the bracelet and treasure box charm. "I told Mrs. Whippie how you'd helped me and that you wanted a bracelet."

Violet shrugged like she didn't care all that much. But after she put the bracelet on, she smiled and said, "It's really pretty. How come you're not wearing yours?"

"I am wearing it," I said, rolling up my sleeve. "I just don't want anyone asking me questions about it."

"Yeah, well, no one will notice it at my house," Violet said. "My dad's busy with other things."

"What things?" I asked, but she didn't answer. Instead, she picked up Mrs. Whippie's letter and read it aloud:

Dear Izzy,

I've enclosed a bracelet and charms for Violet. I'd be honored to have her join my school. I have certainly heard of the Subtle Art of Shutting Up, but I can't say I've practiced it all that much. I greatly prefer the underappreciated genius of Speaking My Mind. I figure if someone doesn't like what I have to say, they shouldn't put their ears in close proximity to my mouth.

What's all this talk of pretty pinkies and sore thumbs? In my opinion, the thumb is much more valuable than the pinky. The pinky, though important, is the window dressing of digits, if you ask me. It's thin, it gets a lot of attention if you hold a teacup incorrectly (pinkies in, you know!), but otherwise, my money is on the

*thumb. Why, most tasks in this world require the use
of two good, strong thumbs.*

*And speaking of tasks, I have two for you this time!
Your hometown sounds lovely, and I found out that
Dandelion Middle School is having their Harvest Dance
this Saturday night. I want you to go to the dance and
enjoy yourself. After that, it's time to make something
beautiful. There are lots of things in this world that
need beautifying. My ankles, for one thing, but that's
a lost cause! Find something that could use a little
sprucing up, and work your magic on it.*

Sincerely,
Mrs. Whippie

"Her letters are so peculiar," Violet said when she finished reading. "And I don't understand all the stuff about
thumbs and pinkies." She looked up. "Is that a metaphor
for something?"

I shrugged instead of answering. The truth was, I
was coming to love Mrs. Whippie's letters. Somewhere
out there in San Francisco, she was reading my words,
and she didn't seem to think I was weird or odd or a late

bloomer (I heard Grandma Bertie tell Aunt Mildred that's what I was right after Aunt Mildred moved in with us). Mrs. Whippie talked about star-spangled sunsets and sore thumbs like they were all perfectly normal. Like *I* was perfectly normal.

"Izzy? Are you around?" Daisy Caulfield's voice floated up from below.

"Put this away," Violet whispered, handing me back the letter. "We can talk about the tasks after Daisy leaves."

"Izzy? Your Mom told me you were back here."

Violet poked her head out the window. "We're up here," she said before I could stop her.

"No!" I whispered. "No one can come up here."

Violet looked around at the star-stickered wall and stood up quickly. "Actually, Daisy, we'll come down to you!"

But it was too late. Daisy was already climbing the ladder and pulling herself up through the hole in the ground. "Izzy, I need to talk to you. I still want that quote from . . ." She stopped when she saw the stickers, which were faintly glowing in the fading afternoon sun, and her eyes widened.

"You?" she said. "*You're* the Star Bandit?"

"No! I just . . . I like star stickers."

Daisy studied me for a second, then shook her head.

"You're lying, I can tell. I know we don't know each other that well, but I never would've thought you'd try to mess up your own mother's campaign."

"I didn't! Look—We cleaned out Ms. Zubov's garden, and the stickers fell out of my backpack, but all that stuff with the campaign materials, that was just an accident."

"*We?*" Daisy glanced at Violet.

"I mean me," I answered quickly. "Me, myself, and I."

Daisy still looked like she didn't believe me. "So you're the Star Bandit, but you *didn't* mean to mess with your mom's stuff? How exactly could that be an accident?"

"Show her Mrs. Whippie's letters," Violet said suddenly.

"What's a Whippie?" Daisy asked.

"Not what, who," Violet said. "I helped Izzy clean the garden, and it's just like she said. It was an accident." To me, Violet said, "You might as well show her."

Silently, I took the letters from the photo box and handed them over to Daisy.

"'A prize unlike any other,'" Daisy repeated as she read the first letter. "What do you think it is?"

"I don't know, but it had better be a darn good one, for all the trouble we might get in," Violet said.

Daisy glanced at Violet over the top of the letter. "Are you in the charm school too?"

Violet held up her wrist with the bracelet. "Yeah, I guess I just joined."

"You're not going to tell anyone, are you?" I asked Daisy after she'd finished reading the last letter. "No one will believe that we cleared out the garden, but that I didn't mean to vandalize anything."

Daisy thought about it for a second. "I guess I won't."

"Thank you. Because if—"

"On one condition." Daisy crossed her arms over her chest.

I stared back at her. "What condition?"

"I came here to try and get that quote from your dad— but now I want something even better. I want to come with you when you do your next two tasks. And I get to interview you afterward, as the Star Bandit."

"That's blackmail," Violet said.

Daisy shrugged. "I call it creative journalism."

"Well, it's still wrong," Violet said, "and I won't—"

"Wait." I put my hand up. "I'll handle this, Violet."

This was serious business. No one could find out I was the Star Bandit. Not until I could figure out a way to fix things with Mom, at least. I could just imagine what people would say if they knew it was me. *Yep, that Izzy Malone, we all knew there was a screw loose somewhere, didn't we?*

Mom would be so embarrassed. I don't think she could even look me in the eyes. Instead, I think she'd spend most of her time trying to convince everyone my screw-ups weren't her fault.

"What's in it for me if I agree?" I asked.

"What do you want?" Daisy asked.

"Um . . ." Okay, so I hadn't gotten that far. I just wanted to say something tough and cool-sounding.

"We want consultation rights," Violet said suddenly.

"What?" Daisy said.

"What are consultation rights?" I asked. I swear, sometimes I wished Violet would just speak plain English.

"It means we insist on reading and editing your article before you publish it," Violet said. "That way we know you'll tell the truth."

Daisy and Violet stared at each other until Daisy sighed. "You're no fun at all, you know that? Okay, fine. You two can look at the article before I turn it in."

"I don't understand why you want to go with me on the next task, though," I said. "Couldn't you just interview me and be done with it?"

"Sure, but let's think big. You perform the task and beautify something, leaving a bunch of your star stickers as your calling card, and I'll write an article about how you were misunderstood. Anonymously, of course—I won't use your actual name. I'll turn you into Dandelion Hollow's version of Robin Hood." Daisy's eyes were glittering with the possibilities, and I had to admit, blackmail aside, I admired her style.

"What do you get out of all this?" I asked.

"Exposure as a journalist. I wanted to be the sixth-grade editor of the *Grapevine*, but they gave it to someone else because I was homeschooled last year. Some girl named Olivia Van something."

"Olivia Vanderberg." Violet nodded. "I know her. She's also president of the Eco Club and on the baton twirling team. She's Ms. Harmer's daughter."

"She is?" Daisy looked surprised. "But they don't have the same last name."

Violet shrugged. "The Hammer went back to her maiden name after she got divorced."

I stared at Violet. For someone she absolutely hated, Violet sure seemed to know a lot about Ms. Harmer.

"Well?" Daisy said, turning back to me. She spit into her hand and stuck it out. "Do we have a deal?"

"Ew, Daisy, that's disgusting," Violet said.

But a little saliva never bothered me, so I spit into my own hand before shaking Daisy's. "Deal," I said.

"Gross," Violet said. "The two of you need serious help with your hygiene."

Daisy ignored that and looked at Mrs. Whippie's latest letter. "Were you originally planning on going to the dance?"

"No. Definitely not." In my opinion, school dances are totally lame. I mean, I've never actually *been* to one, since the Harvest Dance is the first of the year. But how much fun can they really be? They're at school, for one thing. And even though they're held in the gym, you can't play basketball. Plus, there are teachers and parent chaperones all over the place, just waiting to squash any fun you might actually have.

But it looked like if I wanted to earn my charm, I was going to have to go anyway.

"What about the other task?" Daisy said. "What can you beautify?"

"I think we could take care of both tasks at the dance," I said. "Without anyone knowing."

"Like another secret mission?" Violet asked.

I nodded. I had a plan forming. If I needed to beautify something, I was pretty sure I knew exactly what I would do.

17

THE THREE HENS

Everyone in my house has lots of opinions. The trouble is, they all feel perfectly fine invading my room and giving them to me. Mom, Grandma Bertie, and Aunt Mildred didn't like the clothes I'd picked out to wear to the dance tonight. The three of them were standing close to my bed, where I'd stashed my walkie-talkie underneath my old teddy bear, and I didn't want them to find it.

"Well," Grandma Bertie said, squinting, "your outfit is certainly colorful."

I knew what that meant. A lot of times, "colorful" is just code for "unacceptable."

"And you really could do with a haircut," Mom added.

"If you want, we could cut it right now. Think how much easier it would be to brush if it were shorter."

"I'm allergic to scissors," I said, and Mom and Grandma Bertie exchanged exasperated glances. "What's wrong with what I'm wearing right now?" I had on an outfit I had gotten from Dandelion Thrift: a neon yellow shirt and a long orange gauzy skirt. With my combat boots, of course.

"It's perfectly fine," Grandma Bertie said, "if you want to be a crossing guard." She turned to Mom. "Does Izzy have a nice dress she could wear? Like maybe navy blue or beige?"

"Beige? Izzy is eleven, not eleven hundred," Aunt Mildred said, rolling her eyes. I don't think I'd ever seen someone that old roll their eyes.

"Beige is a perfectly normal color," Grandma Bertie argued.

"Normal?" Aunt Mildred looked like Grandma Bertie had just said a cuss word. "What an utterly terrible word—it sucks all the spark and creativity right out of a person. I've simply got no tolerance for people like that."

"Yes, dear," Grandma Bertie said, sighing heavily. "We all know that."

"I don't wear beige," I announced. "Beige is soul-sucking." I'd heard the word "soul-sucking" from Violet—she was

adding it to one of her word lists when I stopped by her
locker yesterday to go over our plan for tonight. "Besides,
girls don't wear dresses to this kind of dance. It's not formal. It's sort of come-as-you-are."

But from the look on Mom's face, going "as I was" just
wasn't going to cut it.

"I'll be chaperoning tonight, Izzy, and everyone
knows I'm running for mayor, and it would really help
me out if—"

Chaperoning?

"Wait, what? *You'll* be at the dance?" I blurted.

This was a serious problem for me. In order to complete my beautification task tonight, I needed to get deep
into the school, which was certain to be off-limits.

"They needed more chaperones. Melanie Harmer
mentioned it when I was talking to her about your poetry
assignment." Mom made it sound like it was *my* fault she'd
been roped into chaperoning.

"And you think I'll make you look bad by wearing
this?" I held out my arms and thought about the photo of
her and Dad and Carolyn sitting at the piano. She could
erase me from her family photo, but she couldn't stick me
in a bland beige dress and erase me from my own school
dance.

Mom ignored me. "I think I have something in my closet that might work," she said to Grandma Bertie, and headed for the door. "I'll be right back."

"You know, dear," Grandma Bertie said after Mom left, "it couldn't hurt to be a little accommodating, just this once. Your mother is working awfully hard on her campaign."

"Well, so what?" Aunt Mildred snapped. "Izzy isn't the one running for mayor."

Times like these, I didn't mind Aunt Mildred, or her cranky attitude. I figured maybe one of these days I should take her up on her offer to visit my old room and chat with her. Just then, my walkie-talkie crackled to life: "Word-nerd to Stargazer, do you copy?"

"Did you hear that?" Grandma Bertie said. "Something just talked." She eyed my teddy bear suspiciously.

"I didn't hear anything, Bertha," Aunt Mildred said. "Maybe you should get a hearing aid."

"*You're* the one who needs a hearing aid," Grandma Bertie retorted.

"Grandma Bertie, Aunt Mildred," I said quickly. "Do either of you have any jewelry I could borrow tonight?" They both looked delighted I'd asked, and after they left to go look, I picked up the walkie-talkie. "I read you,

Wordnerd. But we have a major problem. The Hammer talked my mother into chaperoning tonight."

"Tell me about it." Violet sounded sour. "My dad will be there too."

"We'll figure something out. But I can't talk right now. Over and out." I had just tucked my walkie-talkie back under my teddy bear when Mom returned holding a brown bag. Or maybe it was a dress? Aunt Mildred and Grandma Bertie followed behind her, both of them holding pairs of dangly earrings.

"Isabella," Mom began, "I'm going to have to insist that you—"

"What's going on in here?" Carolyn wandered into the room, followed by her best friend, Layla.

"Everyone is ganging up on me," I said.

"No one is ganging up on you," Mom said.

"Yes, you are. You want me to change everything about myself so I'll look better for your stupid campaign."

"Now, wait just a minute! I never—"

"I'll handle this," Carolyn said. "Everyone out."

That's one thing about being a child prodigy: You can get away with stuff other people can't. If I tried to order everyone out of the room, Mom would tell me to stop being so difficult and disrespectful. But since Carolyn the

Great said it, Mom just threw up her hands and left.

"Go on, Grandma Bertie and Aunt Mildred," Carolyn said, shooing them from the room. "I've got this." She shut the door behind them and said, "So, what's wrong?"

"The usual. Mom doesn't think I'm good enough, so she's trying to change me."

"That's not true." Carolyn shook her head. "Mom doesn't think *she's* good enough, so she's trying to change *herself.* You're just getting in the way of how she's trying to do that."

You know, sometimes I hate having a sister who's really talented, and really smart.

"Whatever. But she's still on my case about my hair and clothes."

"Your hair is pretty crazy," Carolyn agreed.

"Well, *I* like it."

"Fine," Carolyn said. "I don't actually care. I just kicked everyone out because I thought you'd want a break from the three hens."

"The three hens" is what Carolyn secretly calls Mom, Grandma Bertie, and Aunt Mildred. She says it's because they squawk and cluck more than any real chicken she's ever met.

"You really do have nice hair, though," Layla spoke up.

"And you have a pretty face—it's just hidden behind so much hair."

I looked in the mirror. My hair was the color of a toasted bagel, and it hung down nearly to my waist, tangled in knots as usual. I hadn't intentionally set out to grow it so long. One day a couple years ago, Mom was in a cranky mood and said I was way overdue for a haircut. She ordered me into the bathroom so she could chop it off.

"It'll be easier to take care of that way," she had said. "Since you can't ever be bothered to brush it."

"It's *my* hair," I'd answered. "Why should *you* get to decide when it gets cut?" After that, I refused to sit down whenever she brought out the scissors.

"I guess it is a little out of control," I said now.

"We could cut your hair if you want," Carolyn said. "Layla wants to be a hairdresser one day, right, Layla?"

Layla nodded and snapped her gum. "That, or a computer engineer."

"Do you think you can fix Izzy's hair?" Carolyn asked.

Layla turned my chin this way and that, studying my face and hair, before finally nodding again.

Carolyn retrieved Mom's haircutting scissors and handed them to Layla, who told me to sit still.

"Do you have much practice cutting hair?" I asked.

"Loads," Layla answered, taking her first snip. "Just . . . not on actual people."

"What?" My head snapped back.

"Calm down," Carolyn said. "It's not like she could make it any worse."

"Thanks a lot." I stuck my tongue out at Carolyn, who crossed her eyes at me.

"I normally practice on old dolls," Layla said. "But if you don't like it, we can always shave it off. You could say you were making a statement or something."

"A statement about what?" I asked.

"Who knows?" Carolyn said. "But wouldn't you like to see the look on Mom's face if you shaved your head?"

Carolyn and I both thought about that for a second. Then Carolyn frowned and turned to Layla. "Make sure you do a really good job."

Layla began cutting, stopping every few minutes to step back and make sure she wasn't accidentally giving me a Mohawk, I guess. "You missed a spot," Carolyn would say occasionally, or, "Even it out a little more."

After a while Layla put down the scissors and said she was done. She handed me Carolyn's hand mirror. "What do you think?"

My once-long hair was shaped in a spiky sort of bob. Best of all, I'd hardly ever have to brush it. "I like it," I said.

"What about your clothes?" Carolyn asked. "Do you want to change them?"

"I like your look," Layla said. "It's really funky. You stand out a mile away."

I paused while I considered that. Standing out a mile away was about the *last* thing I wanted to do tonight. Not with what I had planned to earn my next charm. Maybe just for one night, I needed something different. Something darker. My eyes fell on Carolyn's black jacket. Something sleeker. And footwear that didn't make a sound.

"Can I borrow that?" I pointed to Carolyn's jacket. "And your black ballet flats? We wear the same size now."

"Sure."

Tonight I needed to blend in. Disappear, even. That way, when the Star Bandit struck again, no one would be the wiser.

CHAPTER 18

COLORING THE WORLD

The only thing more embarrassing than showing up to a school dance alone is showing up with your mother. We were running late because Mom got tied up with campaign stuff, and afterward, she locked herself in her bedroom, where I heard her talking to herself again ("You are powerful, Janine. You are strong . . ."), so the dance had already started by the time we walked into the gym at Dandelion Middle.

"I can't believe this is your first middle school dance," Mom said. "It seems like my own first dance was just yesterday." She flinched, like she'd just remembered something painful. "You know, Isabella, we're not as different as you may think."

"Izzy. And we're not? Really?" I found that hard to believe. Sometimes it seemed like we didn't even live on the same planet.

"Really." She looked like she wanted to say something else, but then seemed to decide against it. Then she was hurrying away to check in with the other chaperones, calling over her shoulder that she hoped I'd have a good time.

Maybe that was a good thing, because she hadn't had time to notice the walkie-talkie or the paintbrush I tucked under Carolyn's jacket, both of which I needed to complete Mrs. Whippie's tasks. Everything else, I'd smuggled into my locker over the last couple days.

I hung back in the doorway and looked around. Tables and chairs had been set up around the edges of the room, leaving the center free for people to dance, although right now everyone just hovered at the edges. The girls were camped out on the left side of the room by the refreshment table talking to their friends, while the boys lounged against the opposite wall, nodding their heads to the pounding music and generally trying to look cool. It was like there was an invisible line drawn down the middle of the room.

If this was what middle school dances were like, I was not about to change my opinion regarding their lameness.

"Hi, Izzy." Austin came up behind me. His brown hair was slicked into spikes, and he was wearing a white collared shirt, complete with a tie. His face was red and frozen in a grimace; it looked like his tie was trying to choke him. "My mom made me come tonight. She said I needed to do more with my life than play basketball and video games. But she did say I could walk home with you if I wanted to leave early."

"My mom said the same thing." I glanced over and saw Tyler Jones making fart noises with his armpit. "And I predict I *will* want to leave early."

Right after I finish my task, I added silently to myself.

Austin looked around the room. "Do you think they'll make boys and girls dance? Together, I mean?"

"I'm not sure; I don't know what the rules are. But I don't think you have to if you don't want to. I dislike touching people with sweaty palms."

"Exactly." He smiled. "I would much rather touch a basketball!"

"Me too."

We high-fived. Then Austin stuck his hands in his pockets and took a deep breath. "So, listen: I'm sorry about what happened in the cafeteria. I'm sorry I called you Toad Girl."

"It's okay. Everyone calls me that." Although, actually, that wasn't true. Violet and Daisy never called me anything but Izzy.

"It's not okay," Austin said, shaking his head. "Tyler was going on and on about you punching me, and I was embarrassed. I'm sorry."

"Why are you even friends with him?" I asked, moving aside for a few other kids who wanted to get into the gym. "He's mean."

Austin shrugged. "We've known each other since kindergarten. It's hard to imagine *not* being friends with him. Anyways . . . I miss playing basketball with you."

"Me too," I said.

"So . . . truce?"

"Truce."

We were standing in the doorway, facing each other. The wind from outside was tickling at my newly exposed neck, which made me feel both excited and nervous. A part of me wanted to stay there and forget about the dance, and Mrs. Whippie's task, and another part of me wanted to run away and hide.

Austin frowned. "You look different," he said.

I patted my hair. "Carolyn's friend gave me a haircut."

"No, it's not that." He squinted at me.

"Different clothes?" I tugged at Carolyn's black jacket.

"No, it's not that." He kept squinting, until he smiled and snapped his fingers. "You're getting shorter!"

I rolled my eyes. "Way to be observant, Austin."

Boys, I swear.

"Austin, Izzy—over here!" Tyler Jones waved at us and made loud kissing noises. Did he think we'd come to the dance . . . *together?*

Austin must have wondered the same thing, because his cheeks reddened to boiling and he muttered, "See you," before practically running for the right side of the room.

I turned left and smiled as I passed by Sophia Ramos, who waved at me. I was looking for Daisy and Violet, but unfortunately, I ran into Stella the Terrible first. Her lips were pursed, and she was glancing around the room, her hands fluttering nervously at her sides.

"Hello, Izzy. Have you seen Lauren?"

"No, I haven't," I said, surprised. "I think that's one of the only times in almost two years you've called me Izzy, instead of Toad Girl."

"My mom told me I need to be nice to you because

you're weird and you don't have any friends," Stella said, still glancing around the room.

Nice. "Actually, that's not true," I said.

Because all of a sudden, I realized it wasn't. Stella wasn't the only one looking for someone; I was looking for Violet and Daisy—didn't they count as friends? After all, what else do you call two people who've promised to help you sneak into school and perform a secret task?

Accomplices, maybe. But also friends.

Stella spotted Lauren and the Paddlers and, with a relieved sigh, hurried off to join them. I found Violet sitting at a table, writing a new list in her journal:

Words That Annoy Me:
Punch
Dances
Chaperones
Tyler Jones

"Where's Daisy?" I asked, sitting down next to her.

"Casing the joint," Violet replied, not looking up from her list. "She's trying to figure out the best way to get you inside."

I hadn't told Daisy and Violet exactly what I was

planning. I just told them I needed to get into the school. I figured that gave them plausible deniability if I was caught. Although I wasn't too worried about getting caught this time. After all, I was only trying to beautify something.

Violet looked up from her journal. "Wow. I *love* your hair."

"Thanks. Have you been here long?"

Violet rolled her eyes. "Since an hour before it started. My dad decided since he was a chaperone we needed to be here early."

I followed her gaze. Mr. Barnaby was standing near the sound system, nodding his head to the music. When he caught sight of us staring at him, he waved.

"He's been looking over here every two seconds," Violet complained. "I don't know how you're going to get away."

"He's not our biggest problem," Daisy said, sitting down on the other side of Violet. She glanced over at me. "Nice hair, Izzy. . . . Okay, first, we have the politicians"— she pointed to Mom and Mayor Franklin, both of whom were smiling tightly while Principal Chilton talked to them—"Mayor Franklin's in a really cranky mood— she's been yelling at students over the tiniest things— and as soon as Izzy's mom got here, she joined right in.

I think they're having a silent contest over who can be the strictest chaperone. Principal Chilton is actually telling them both to tone it down. Also, the school is locked up tight from the outside. The only way in is through the double doors leading from here into the library hall. So right now, our biggest problem is the Hammer. Look."

Ms. Harmer had planted herself in front of the double doors like a sentry on watch. She was yelling at an eighth-grade boy and girl huddling in the corner to get away from each other.

Violet added "Hammer" to her list of annoying words, and I said, "We'll worry about her in a minute." I turned back to Violet. "Do you have your bracelet with you?"

She nodded and patted her jeans pocket. We'd both agreed we'd follow Mrs. Whippie's instructions to the letter. As soon as I completed the task, we could add both the jukebox and paint palette charms to our bracelet. My part of the task was to actually do the beautifying. Violet and Daisy's part was to keep an eye out and alert me if someone was coming my way.

"What do you need us to do?" Daisy asked as we all stared at the Hammer.

"We need to get her away from the door somehow,"

I said, thinking hard. "We need to create some kind of distraction."

Just then, Mr. Barnaby walked by Ms. Harmer. He briefly took her hand and squeezed it, then kept on going.

I'm pretty sure my jaw hit the floor.

"What. Was. *That?*" Daisy asked.

We both turned to stare at Violet, who shrugged glumly. "She and my dad are dating."

"Your dad is dating the Hammer?" Daisy asked, wide-eyed.

"They have been for a while, but they don't want anyone to know yet. That's why I stole her keys. I wasn't supposed to be in her class, but somehow the request got lost, and when class schedules came out they didn't want to make a big deal about it." Tears filled Violet's eyes. "I got so sick of listening to her every day—I had to do something to get away from her."

"I'm so sorry, Violet." I pulled a crumpled tissue out of my pocket and handed it to her.

"Hey . . ." Daisy smiled mischievously. "I've got the perfect way to make Violet feel a whole lot better, *and* get Izzy past those doors."

"How?" I asked.

"Never underestimate the power of the press." Daisy

turned to Violet. "Do you have your walkie-talkie?" she asked, and Violet nodded. "Good. The two of you go and wait by the refreshment table. Izzy, as soon as Ms. Harmer moves, make a run for it."

"Yes, sir." I saluted, and a couple girls passing by gave me strange looks. After Violet and I stationed ourselves behind the punch bowl, Daisy marched up to the double doors and stopped in front of Ms. Harmer. She timed it perfectly. Right as she yelled, "I saw Mr. Barnaby holding your hand. Are you two dating?" the music ended abruptly.

The room went silent. Ms. Harmer paled. "Daisy, you're being inappropriate. My private life is just that: private, and none of your business."

"I disagree." Daisy produced a pen and a small notepad from her pocket. "I think the readers of the *Grapevine* have a right to know your intentions concerning Dandelion Hollows' youngest widower." She clicked her pen. "Care to comment?"

"Daisy, you're making a scene." Ms. Harmer glanced around the room. Every face stared back at her. Except for Mr. Barnaby, who was frantically gesturing to the sound guy and telling him to start the music again.

"It's okay if you don't want to comment, Ms. Harmer.

I'll just go and ask Mr. Barnaby." With that, Daisy spun on her heel and waded through the crowd. "Mr. Barnaby! Can I talk to you?"

"Daisy—wait!" Ms. Harmer took off after her, just as the music started up again.

"Go!" Violet said. "Call me on your walkie if you need anything."

Quickly, I slid through the doors, the music fading behind me as I walked down the corridor, excitement building within me. This was it! Operation Earn Your Charm was on!

The can of paint and the towel I was using as a drop cloth were both still in my locker, undisturbed. The paint was orange; not an exact match to the orange underneath the gray wall near the library, but close enough. I'd found it in Mom's craft closet in the garage.

In no time I had everything set up. I dipped the brush in the can and hoped my fellow students would be so excited when they came to school on Monday. Ever since I'd read Mrs. Whippie's third letter I'd known that if I had to beautify something, it was going to be this wall. It seemed to me that the old orange paint was just bursting to get out, trapped as it was underneath all that boring gray. Maybe if I showed everyone how beautiful this wall could be, it would convince them to do away with all the gray walls at Dandelion Middle. Maybe one day there would be no more gray walls, ever!

It was a small wall, just a connecting section between two longer walls, so it didn't take too long, and I used a stepladder from the janitor's closet to reach the upper half. I waited for the paint to dry (mostly, anyway) then stuck some star stickers in the middle.

A little color to brighten everyone's day, courtesy of the Star Bandit!

I quickly washed the brush off in the girls' bathroom and stowed it and the paint can and towel back in my locker—I'd smuggle it all home on Monday. When I was finished, I took the walkie-talkie and signaled Violet:

"Stargazer to Wordnerd, do you copy?"

A few seconds later, the walkie squawked to life. "I copy, Stargazer."

"Mission accomplished. Am I clear to reenter the gym?"

"Negative, Stargazer. The extraction point is blocked. Stand by for instructions."

I waited for a few minutes and wondered exactly how Violet was going to get the Hammer away from the double doors again.

"Stargazer, this is Storybreaker, do you copy?" This time it was Daisy on the other end.

"Storybreaker?"

"If you and Violet can have code names, then so can I," Daisy answered impatiently. "Stargazer, proceed immediately to the extraction point. The way has been temporarily cleared."

I hurried up the hallway and slid back through the double doors, hoping no one would notice me. I needn't have worried, though. The night was back in full swing, and the dance floor was crowded. Violet was over by the punch table, helping a shaken-looking Ms. Harmer clean up several spilled cups, loudly apologizing for knocking them over. Daisy was helping them, and Mrs. Menzel, the school librarian, was saying she'd go to the janitor's closet for cleaning supplies. I figured I should stay away from Ms. Harmer, so I skirted the edge of the room. A slow song was playing, and I stared out at the dance floor.

Austin was slow dancing with Stella Franklin.

All at once I felt like crying. Or yelling at Austin. I wasn't sure which, and I wasn't sure why. What did I care if Austin wanted to dance with Stella the Terrible? Except . . . a part of me wondered why, if Austin wanted to slow dance with someone, didn't he ask *me*?

Wait . . . did that mean I actually *wanted* to slow dance with Austin?

My face felt flushed, and my insides felt all tingly and twisty. . . . Did that mean I had a *crush* on Austin? I considered the signs:

> a. My palms were sweaty.
> b. My heart was racing.
> c. I felt like I might puke at any moment.
> d. I also felt a nearly uncontrollable urge to punch both Austin and Stella in the face.

Darn it!

I guess some girls might be excited to discover they had their first crush. But I just wanted to run away and never come back to school ever again.

"Where have you been?" Daisy appeared next to me, Violet at her side. "We've been looking for you."

"I've been right here," I said, watching Austin and Stella. "I've been here this whole time."

Did Austin have a crush on Stella? Maybe crushes were like that big sinkhole at the edge of town: They just opened up one day out of nowhere, and if you didn't watch your step, you could fall right into them. Maybe Austin had fallen into a crush, and Stella had just happened to be standing there when it happened.

How *did* these things happen?

"So?" Violet said. "It's done?"

I pulled my gaze away from Austin and Stella. "It's done."

Violet nodded, and together we pulled out our bracelets and charms. "Ready?" Violet asked.

"Ready," I said.

We both paused; it felt like a formal moment. "We have earned our charms," I said solemnly, and we began hooking them onto the gold chain. Then we held out our wrists. The charms seemed to catch the light and shine. I felt my chest lighten, and I decided not to think about Austin and his terrible taste in dance partners.

"When am *I* going to get a bracelet?" Daisy grumbled. "I want to be a part of your charm school too."

"I'll write Mrs. Whippie a letter tonight," I said.

"Those are really pretty bracelets," said a voice behind us.

I turned around and saw Sophia Ramos. She was wearing her dark brown hair back in sparkly barrettes and was staring at us tentatively, like she wasn't sure she should come any closer.

"They are, aren't they?" Daisy said. "And I don't even *like* jewelry."

"Where did you get them?" Sophia asked, seeming encouraged. "Because they look a lot like—"

"He's done it again! The Star Bandit was here!"

We all turned to see Mrs. Menzel come bursting through the double doors. Her face was purple, and a few hairs had sprung loose from her bun. The sound was cut, and the room went silent.

"What do you mean?" Ms. Harmer said, putting an arm around Mrs. Menzel.

"I went . . . to the janitor's closet . . . by the library," Mrs. Menzel wheezed. "He tugged it. . . . He left star stickers all over the place."

Ms. Harmer, along with Mom, Mayor Franklin, and several students, pushed through the doors to go get a look. Violet and Daisy turned to me, uncertain expressions on their faces.

"Mrs. Menzel seems pretty upset," Violet whispered. "What is she talking about? What did you do?"

"Nothing," I said, glancing meaningfully at Sophia, who was staring at us.

But Violet didn't seem to notice or care. "Izzy, what did you *do*?"

"I painted a wall orange," I said. "I don't see what the big deal is."

"That's brilliant!" Daisy said. "That's a way better story than I ever could have hoped for. . . . 'The Star Bandit Strikes Again!'" She framed the headlines with her hands. "Or how about, 'He's Back!'"

"Are you two crazy?" Violet said. "Izzy, I thought you were going to clean up the bathroom or something. You mean you vandalized a wall?"

"I painted the wall. There's a big difference. Aren't you sick of staring at puke-gray walls?"

"Puke isn't gray," Daisy put in. She wrinkled her nose. "Unless maybe you've just eaten rotten oatmeal."

Violet looked like *she* was about to puke. "Do you know how much trouble we could get into?" she whispered furiously. "Dad is still mad at me for stealing the Hammer's keys, and neither of them are in a good mood right now after the stunt Daisy just pulled—"

"Hey, wait a minute!" Daisy said.

"—and if they find out I helped you vandalize something—"

"I wasn't trying to vandalize anything. I was trying to—"

"To beautify it, I *know*! But only a chronically weird person would think—"

Violet clapped a hand over her mouth, but it was too late. The word "weird" ping-ponged between us. It felt like an arrow every time it hit me.

"Who are you calling 'weird'?" I said. "You forget I've been to your house—you painted your bedroom walls purple!"

At the other end of the room, a commotion was steadily growing. Mom and Ms. Harmer returned to the gym. Mom appeared to be issuing instructions to Principal Chilton and Mr. Barnaby. Candidate Malone to the rescue. I wondered if it had occurred to her that she could snag a few extra votes if she handled this well.

"Izzy, I'm sorry," Violet said. "I didn't mean—"

"You guys can talk about this later." Sophia, who had been silently watching us all this time, spoke up. She leaned in and lowered her voice. "Izzy, there's orange paint on your shoes."

I looked down and, sure enough, a splatter of orange dots marched over Carolyn's black ballet flats.

Violet and Daisy glanced at each other, and they seemed to make a silent decision. "Go home, Izzy," Violet whispered. She glanced at Sophia. "Before someone notices your shoes and says something to a teacher."

Sophia stared back at her. "I'm not going to say anything."

"I'm not supposed to walk home by myself," I said. "My mom said I could either wait until she was done chaperoning, or I could walk home with Austin Jackson."

But walking home with Austin was no longer an option. Not with orange paint splashed on my shoes. And definitely not when I might possibly have a crush on him. In fact, it was debatable whether or not I was ever going to speak to him again.

Sophia stepped forward. "I'll walk you home." She glanced over at Violet. "And I won't say anything to anyone, I promise."

"Are you sure?" Violet said.

Sophia nodded. "I'll call my mom on my cell and have her pick me up from Izzy's house." She paused, and added, "She'll be happy I actually talked to someone tonight."

While other students clustered into groups, excitedly talking about the Star Bandit, Sophia and I quietly left and headed for my house. I didn't understand why everyone was getting so upset.

After all, I was just trying to bring a little more color to the world.

CHAPTER
19
ODD VISION

Dear Mrs. Whippie,

I completed the third task, but like the one before, it didn't quite go as planned. I went to the dance like you asked me to, and I tried really hard to beautify something, but all most people saw was an awkward pile of messiness that didn't fit in anywhere.

Kind of like me.

People say I'm weird, and right now I'm beginning to think they're right. You know how some animals have

*night vision? Well, maybe I have odd vision. Maybe
that's why I feel so different from everyone else all the
time. Maybe it's because I really do see things differently.
I painted a wall, and I thought it was the greatest thing
ever. But Violet and everyone at school is really upset. I
guess I just don't understand why a bunch of gray walls
are okay and one tiny orange wall is vandalism.*

*Anyway, Violet and I aren't speaking right now. I'm
really mad at her, and I honestly don't know if we're
still friends. But I sure do appreciate your charms, and
I'm looking forward to your next letter.*

*Also, my friend Daisy would like a bracelet and charms
too. Is that okay?*

*Your Friend,
Izzy Malone*

*P.S.: Daisy and I are wondering what "a prize unlike
any other" means. Does it mean money? If so, I'd like
you to know we prefer cash.*

20

EXTRA, EXTRA! READ ALL ABOUT IT!

Dandelion Gazette Special Edition:

The Star Bandit Strikes Again!
by Daisy Caulfield
(Article first appeared in the *Grapevine*,
Dandelion Middle's student-run newspaper)

This weekend the students at Dandelion Middle got more than stale cookies and watered-down punch at their annual Harvest Dance. Turns out, they had front-row seats to the site of the Star Bandit's second target: a wall in the library hall, which the Star Bandit—your favorite troublemaker and mine—decided to paint a disarming orange color. Star stickers were stuck to the wall to make sure everyone knew who was responsible.

The site was discovered by Mrs. Menzel, Dandelion Middle's longtime librarian. "I couldn't believe it," Mrs. Menzel said, fanning herself at the memory. "An orange wall. Can you imagine?"

Indeed, many people *could* imagine it, and they were none too happy.

"It's a disgusting display of vandalism," Kendra Franklin, current mayor of Dandelion Hollow, is quoted as saying. "The Star Bandit is a selfish nuisance, and a disgrace to our community. I want to know how Chief Malone is handling the situation, because right now it appears he's doing nothing."

Of course, not everyone thinks the Star Bandit is a nuisance.

"I don't see what everyone is getting so upset about," said Coco Martin, a guidance counselor at Dandelion Middle. "I think it's fantastic—I wish all the walls at this school were painted orange. Does anyone know if the Star Bandit is accepting orders? Star Bandit, if you're reading this, feel free to come and paint my office. I want a beautiful wall too."

But though some think the wall beautiful, the Star Bandit's artistry may have had an unintended effect: The school budget, which, according to Richard Chilton, principal of Dandelion Middle, is stretched "tight to darn-near strangling," didn't anticipate the cleanup costs associated with the Star Bandit's efforts. His comments prompted sixth-grade student Olivia Vanderberg, president of Dandelion Middle's Eco Club, to donate club funds for the paint removal. But this move has others grumbling too, as those monies were said to be designated for a class trip to Dandelion Observatory later in the year.

"I really wish the Star Bandit had thought through the consequences of his actions," Principal Chilton is quoted as saying.

Whether or not the Star Bandit—whose identity still remains a mystery—is given to self-reflection is unknown, but others have seen his growing notoriety as an opportunity to drum up business. Don Donaldson, owner of Don's Donuts, has just announced he will be serving star donuts starting tomorrow.

"I've already got two dozen orders!" he exclaimed. "Thank you, Star Bandit!"

21

ORANGE IS
THE NEW AWESOME

"I can't believe that woman," Mom said a few evenings later as she put down her copy of the *Dandelion Gazette*. She had just finished reading Daisy's article. "Kendra knows darn well your father is doing everything he can to catch the Star Bandit. She's just trying to make our family look bad."

"Mmmhmm," I said, because it seemed the safest response. And also because my mouth was full of pancakes. We were having breakfast for dinner that night. Dad was still at the station, and Carolyn had a guitar lesson, so it was just me, Mom, Grandma Bertie, and Aunt Mildred.

"I think it's exciting," Grandma Bertie said. "Izzy, did you see anything at the dance? The Knatterers are meeting tonight, and they're all dying to know."

I swallowed my pancake and kept my eyes on my plate. "I think—"

"I think it's unconscionable," Aunt Mildred said.

"I agree," Grandma Bertie said. "That Star Bandit—"

"Not the Star Bandit!" Aunt Mildred pounded her fist on the table. "The way you and your Knatterers are just out there begging for town gossip!"

While they bickered, I chewed my pancakes silently. Since my plan to beautify the school didn't quite go over the way I hoped, Daisy decided it was too risky to interview me, so she'd written something more straightforward. The words "disarming," "artistry," and "monies" came from Violet, who helped Daisy write the article. Violet insisted on it after she read Daisy's first draft, which featured a bunch of juicy bits about her dad dating Ms. Harmer. Violet made her take it all out. But gossip travels lightning fast in Dandelion Hollow, so everyone already knew anyway. Mom had been going on and on earlier about how scandalous it was, and how maybe if Ms. Harmer weren't so busy cozying up to Violet's dad, maybe the Star Bandit wouldn't have slipped right under her nose.

"Kendra's right about one thing, though," Mom added.

I swallowed. "Oh, yeah? What's that?"

"That Star Bandit is a disgrace. What a ridiculous idea, painting that wall."

"I think the wall looks nice." I'd meant to keep my mouth shut, but, big surprise, I was finding it harder than I'd thought. "A lot of people were taking selfies in front of it today, before it gets covered up."

That was the thing I just couldn't believe. After all the trouble I went to, they were just going to cover it up again. Principal Chilton gave the school janitor the donated funds from the Eco Club to purchase new gray paint. Out with the orange, in with the dull gray.

"Novelty always attracts attention," Mom said. "But it's still vandalism."

"Well, I think it's awesome. Orange is the new awesome."

"How can you think it looks good?" Mom demanded. "The Star Bandit did an absolutely terrible job. He got paint all over the floor."

I bit into a buttery biscuit before I said something that gave me away. Everyone was still convinced the Star Bandit was some kind of vandal—a teenage boy, probably—which was helpful, and also really annoying.

But I did feel bad that the members of the Eco Club were going to miss their trip to the observatory, and I knew I was going to have to come clean—just as soon as I figured out how to make it up to everyone.

We ate for a few minutes in silence; but like usual, my mouth could only stay shut for so long. "Don't you think orange is way better than gray. Gray is insipid." I'd gotten the word "insipid" from Violet back when we were still speaking to each other.

"Gray is a perfectly respectable color," Mom said. "Orange, on the other hand, is loud and out of place."

"Just because something is respectable," I said, "doesn't mean it's interesting."

"And just because something is interesting," Mom countered, "doesn't mean it's acceptable."

Mom and I stared at each other, and all of a sudden, I could tell we weren't fighting over colors anymore.

"Oh, yeah? Well, maybe gray could learn a thing or two from orange," I said. "Like how to have some fun once in a while."

Grandma Bertie and Aunt Mildred were glancing back and forth between us, both of them seemingly afraid to say anything.

"Maybe orange could learn how to fit in once in a

while," Mom said, her voice tightening. "Instead of making gray's life so hard."

"Or maybe gray could learn orange *doesn't want* to fit in."

"Maybe orange should clear the table and take out the trash, as it's her turn tonight."

"Fine." I pushed back my chair and stood up. "I was finished anyway."

After the dishes were done I took the trash and headed outside. The night was clear. Orion and Big D were shining. Ready, as always, to listen. "She's never going to understand me," I said.

I could swear the tip of Big D's handle winked at me, like he was nodding in agreement.

BOBBLEHEADS

On Thursday, I decided I needed to track down Sophia Ramos. With everyone up in arms over the Star Bandit, I needed to make sure she was exercising her constitutional right to remain silent. That meant I needed to send myself on a sensitive diplomatic mission to find her. And *that* meant I was stuck visiting the cafeteria again.

On the way in, I ran into Daisy, who was balancing a tray of questionable-looking burritos.

"What are you doing here?" I asked.

"What do you mean, what am I doing here? It's a cafeteria. People eat in cafeterias. Although most days I usually take my tray back to the *Grapevine* office." Daisy made it sound like it was a suite or something, but the *Grapevine* office was just a small unused classroom in the English hall.

"So you don't usually eat here either?"

"I almost did, once." Daisy shrugged. "But I didn't know where to sit. What are you doing here? Don't you usually eat under that one tree?"

"I need to talk to Sophia about . . . you know."

Daisy nodded. "Damage control, right."

"You want to come?" I asked.

"Sure. You can share my burritos with me if you don't want to wait in line. Do you think Violet should join us?"

"Violet and I aren't speaking." Ever since the dance, we'd been avoiding each other. Or I was avoiding *her*, at least.

"Here." Daisy shoved her tray into my hands. She pulled her cell phone from her pocket and began tapping at the screen. "I'm texting her."

Pretty soon, Daisy's screen lit up with Violet's response. "She's on her way." Daisy put her phone away and took back her tray.

When Violet arrived, she wouldn't look me in the eyes. "Hi, Izzy," she said, staring at the floor.

"I'm surprised you came," I said. "I thought I was too *chronically weird* for you to hang out with."

"Izzy," Daisy warned. "Play nice."

"Why? *She's* not playing nice, so why should I?"

"Izzy, I really am sorry—" Violet began.

"Whatever," I said, turning away to look for Sophia. "It's not like I care, anyway."

Except . . . I did care. Every time someone called me "odd" or "weird," I cared, even if I tried hard to act like I didn't. Especially when I thought Violet and I were finally starting to become friends again. But maybe we weren't. Maybe Violet just liked Mrs. Whippie's bracelet and charms so much she was even willing to hang out with Toad Girl.

Daisy and Violet followed me silently as I threaded my way through the cafeteria. I found Sophia eating alone at that empty table behind the Paddlers.

"Hi," I said.

"Hi." She smiled at us as we all took seats around her, which I took to be a good sign.

"Ribbit, ribbit," Stella called from her table.

Sophia glanced their way and frowned, but said nothing.

"How do you like Dandelion Hollow?" I asked.

"It's okay." Her voice was friendly, but her eyes were as watchful as a guard dog's. I think she knew exactly why we were here.

"Just okay?" It occurred to me that in the crowded caf-eteria, Sophia was eating alone. Again.

Sophia nodded. "It's a beautiful town, and a lot less crowded than San Francisco—where I used to live." She paused and raised her eyebrows, as if to say, *Okay, let's get on with it.*

So I got down to business: "Here's the thing: My dad is the chief of police, and my mom is running for mayor."

"I know who your parents are."

"Then you know I will get into an epic amount of trouble if I get caught."

Violet nodded seriously. "I know Izzy's parents. She may not live to see the seventh grade." Violet smiled ten-tatively at me, but I ignored her and stared at Sophia.

"I told you I wouldn't say anything, and I meant it," Sophia said. "But why did you do it? I mean, do you want your mom to lose?"

"No, I definitely want her to win." I may not have understood why Mom wanted to be mayor—most days, I didn't understand anything at all about her—but that didn't mean I wanted her to lose. "I'm going to come clean eventually—"

"You are?" Daisy interrupted, looking surprised.

"Yes—once I figure out a way to make things right.

I just . . . It's all just been a misunderstanding. I never meant to cause so much trouble." I took a deep breath, getting ready to give Sophia all the reasons why I wasn't an apprentice training to get my picture plastered over a WANTED sign.

"Okay," Sophia said, "I believe you."

"You believe me?" I repeated. "Just like that?"

"Yeah, why not? You don't strike me as a mean person, Izzy."

I didn't know what to say to that. It wasn't often that someone took me at my word.

"Well," I said finally, "I guess it's not so much that people think I'm mean, it's that they think I'm weird." I looked pointedly at Violet. "*A lot* of people think I'm weird."

"But I *don't* think that," Violet burst out. "I feel terrible about the other night. What I said was mean and stupid—I was just afraid of getting in trouble. I promise, I don't think you're weird. Please, please, can we forget I said it?"

Violet's eyes looked like shiny sea glass, and I guessed when I really thought about it, I couldn't be too mad at her for saying something stupid. My own foot had been known to take long, extended vacations in my big mouth.

"I missed you," Violet added, as Daisy and Sophia

watched us. "While my mom was sick, and afterward. I guess I just didn't know how to be a friend then. But I missed you."

"I missed you too," I said finally. "Friends?"

"Friends."

Things still felt slightly awkward between us. I guess rebuilding a friendship took time, even if it was something both of us wanted. We weren't the same girls who used to play in my treehouse. I was Toad Girl, Violet was the girl who'd lost her mother, and the last couple years had been hard for both of us.

"Ribbit, ribbit," Stella said from the Paddlers' table.

I turned around to look at her. Generally speaking, I have never wondered if a burrito would make a good football. But when I picked one up off Daisy's plate, I couldn't help thinking how nicely it fit in my hand—and how spectacular it would look plastered all over Stella the Terrible's face. Unfortunately, self-control got the better of me, and I set it back down. I didn't want another cafeteria incident, or another trip to Coco Martin's office.

"*I* think you're weird," Daisy said, staring at me earnestly. "But that's what I like about you. Unlike *some* people." She glanced in the direction of the Paddlers and scowled. "Stella Franklin is the most normal person I've ever met. That's her biggest problem. I mean, *look* at all of them, nodding at whatever Lauren says. They're like a bunch of bobbleheads. I'm surprised they haven't sprained their necks."

"O-*kay*," Sophia said, glancing between the three of us and looking thoroughly confused. "But, Izzy, I still don't understand why you cleaned out the garden and painted the wall."

I rolled up my sleeve to show her my charm bracelet. "Because of this."

Sophia's brow furrowed. "Because of your bracelet?"

I nodded. "Last week I was earning my charm." I gave the paint palette charm a little flick. "I had to beautify something before I could put it on my bracelet, and I thought I'd paint the wall near the library." I shrugged. "But I guess not everyone liked it."

Sophia still looked confused, so I spent the next fifteen minutes explaining Mrs. Whippie's charm school to her. After I finished, she said, "So you have to do something before you can put on the charms she sends you? That is so cool. Are Daisy and Violet members?"

"Sort of, yeah. Violet has a bracelet, and Daisy will probably get hers the next time Mrs. Whippie sends me a letter."

"Do you think I could join?" Sophia asked.

"Um . . ." I glanced at Violet and Daisy, who both nodded. "Sure. Maybe you could help us with the next task, and then I could ask Mrs. Whippie if she'll send you a bracelet?"

"That would be great." Sofia smiled widely. "You know," she added, "at first I thought you got your bracelets from my mother's shop."

"What shop?" I asked.

"My mom owns Charming Trinkets." Sophia frowned. "You've heard of it, right? The jewelry store that opened a couple months ago? It's just a bit down the street from the Kaleidoscope Café."

"Oh, is that what that new store is?" Violet said. "I thought it was another antique shop."

Sophia's shoulders seemed to slump. "Yeah, business hasn't been that great. I told my mom the window display was confusing."

"I send my letters to San Francisco," I said.

"Ribbit, ribbit," someone said from the Paddlers' table.

"That is so annoying," Sophia said. "Why do they keep saying that?"

"It's nothing," I said, feeling my cheeks flushing. "Just forget about it."

"It's something people say to Izzy when her back is turned." Violet shot me a tentative look. "They call her Toad Girl."

As if on cue, Stella said, "Ribbit, ribbit!"

Sophia stared at her for a moment before wiping her hands on her napkin. Then she stood up, all graceful-like, and loudly addressed the Paddlers: "SHUT. UP!"

A few kids sitting nearby snickered. Violet and Daisy stared at her in disbelief. Lauren's mouth dropped open.

"Geez," Stella said. "I was just kidding. You don't have to be so sensitive."

Sophia sat back down like nothing at all had happened, and quietly resumed eating her lunch.

CHAPTER 23

BOY-CRAZY ALIENS

Every time I saw Austin at school, I turned and walked the other way. Just catching a glimpse of him was enough to make my cheeks flush and my heart speed up, leading me to conclude that what I had suspected at the dance was true: I had fallen into my first crush.

I didn't know whether to be excited or seriously annoyed.

One day a girl is all normal, and then—BOOM!—the next she's turned into a boy-crazy alien and starts doing stupid stuff like constantly slipping her crush's name into a conversation, or finding excuses to drop by his locker.

I had no intention of turning into an alien, and I was

determined to not talk about Austin and to go on ignoring him, possibly for the rest of my life. But that didn't work out so well, because the day after Sophia asked to join Mrs. Whippie's charm school, I found myself only a few feet behind him as we walked home from school.

He had his basketball with him, and kept trying to twirl it on his index finger. The ball kept tipping off, though, and he'd have to go chasing after it. When we reached our street, the ball tipped backward and rolled right in front of me. I picked it up and tossed it to him.

Austin grinned. "I came by last night to see if you wanted to play a game of half-court and your mom said you weren't feeling well. Were you sick?"

"I had a cold," I lied. After all, I couldn't exactly tell Austin I was ignoring him because I liked him. Which, when you think about it, doesn't make any sense.

"Are you feeling better now?" he asked as we reached his house.

"Sure," I said, although maybe I was still lying, because my mouth was dry and my stomach was somersaulting. Why didn't anyone ever tell me that having a crush was a little like having the flu?

"Great!" Austin dropped his backpack on the lawn and said, "Want to shoot some hoops?"

"Now?" I asked.

"Sure, why not? We could have a free throw contest."

I looked up at Austin—I swore he'd grown even taller since the dance—and decided that the biggest difference between having the flu and having a crush is that with a crush, sometimes you don't want to get better.

I set my backpack down next to Austin's. We hadn't had a free throw contest in a long time. I was the current reigning champ; last summer, I sank ten baskets in a row.

Austin let me go first, but the ball bounced off the rim.

"Better luck next time," he said, and picked up the ball.

His first try swished right through the basket. So did his second. And his third, fourth, and fifth. "Oh, yeah!" he hollered as he sank his sixth. "Looks like someone's got some skills!"

"Oh, yeah?" I said. "Who would that be?" Austin always got a little annoying when he was winning; and crush or not, I didn't feel like putting up with his declarations of athletic superiority.

"Oh come on, you know I'm better at making free throws than you are—you just got lucky that one time. . . . Yes!" He pumped his fist in the air. "Lucky number seven! . . . So what happened to you at the dance?" he asked as he set up his next shot. "I thought we were supposed to walk home together."

I bent down and pretended to retie my shoe. "I got bored and wanted to leave," I said. "You looked pretty busy dancing with Stella, so I took off."

Oops. I promised myself I wasn't going to mention Stella.

"What does Stella have to do with anything?" he said as he sank the next basket. That was number eight, and if he kept this up, he was on his way to a new record, which just made me even more annoyed.

"Nothing," I said. "I just didn't think you'd be interested in a girl like Stella."

All right, that's it, Izzy. If you don't shut your mouth, I'll duct tape it for you.

"What are you even talking about?" he said, sinking number nine.

"Nothing," I said again. "I just didn't think you wanted to dance with girls."

"I didn't. But the Hammer was freaking out about everyone knowing she's dating Violet's dad and she practically threatened to give us all detention if we didn't start dancing." He sank another basket. "Oh, yeah!" he yelled, throwing his hands in the air. "I have just tied you! One more, baby, and it's a new world record!"

"Awesome," I said. "Any time you want to let me have a turn, just let me know."

"Don't be such a sore loser. I let you go first. It's not my fault you missed."

I begged to differ. I was pretty sure if I wasn't stuck in a crush I would have made my first shot, and I wouldn't be sitting here watching Austin sink basket after basket, like I didn't have anything better to do with my time.

"Where were you, anyway?" he asked as he dribbled the ball a couple times. "I didn't see you on the dance floor."

"Uh . . . I was busy."

"Busy . . . doing what?" He raised the ball to take aim.

I definitely didn't want Austin wondering too hard where I was during the dance, so I said, "For your information, I was dancing with someone too."

Austin's shot bounced hard off the backboard, and the ball rolled into the street.

"Ha!" I said. "There will be no new world records today! I am still the reigning champion! I invite you to call me Queen Izzy."

"You were dancing?" Austin turned to look at me. "With who?"

"An eighth grader," I said, thinking fast. "You don't know him."

"What's his name?"

"What's it matter to you?"

"It doesn't matter to me. You just sound like you're lying."

"How would you know I was lying? Or don't you think anyone would want to dance with Toad Girl?"

"I didn't say that. I just didn't see you dancing with anyone."

"Oh yeah, well, you were probably too busy dancing with Stella the Terrible to notice. Did you actually *look* for me on the dance floor?"

"Yes, I did, okay? Ms. Harmer practically forced me to dance with someone, and I tried to find you, and you weren't anywhere, and I got stuck dancing with Stella. Why are you acting so weird all of a sudden?"

"I don't know," I said. "Maybe you should go ask Stella."

"Whatever, Izzy, I'm going inside." He picked up his backpack. "Sometimes I really don't understand girls," he mumbled as he walked away.

I couldn't blame him. These days, I didn't understand myself much either.

CHAPTER 24

TACKY FAVORITISM

On Saturday, Dad and I were up bright and early, packing picnic lunches to take to Dandelion Lake. With Pumpkin Palooza only a week away, he decided we needed to step up our training sessions.

"It's not enough to be fast," he said as we loaded his kayak onto his truck. "You have to be precise and strong." He picked up a couple tote bags stuffed with rocks and shoved them in behind the kayak.

"What are those for?" I asked.

"You'll see. Let's get moving—Mom said she'd drop by to watch you after Carolyn's through with her rehearsal."

Dad has been taking me to Dandelion Lake ever since

I could walk. After Mom discovered Carolyn's emerging musical genius, their Saturdays were full of lessons, leaving me and Dad alone.

"I haven't got a musical bone in my body," Dad once said. "But I know how to row. The lake, Izzy, that's where I hear music."

I can't say I heard any music as we unloaded the kayak at the aquatic center, but I did hear the students from Dandelion High's rowing team warming up for their practice session.

That's another reason I want to join the Paddlers: You do a couple years with them and you've got a good shot at joining the high school team.

The Paddlers themselves were also practicing at the opposite end of the lake. Dad and I stopped to watch them. They were in individual kayaks, cutting through the lake the way eagles cut through sky. (All of them except for Stella, who struggled a few strokes behind.)

"They look really good," I said.

"They'd look a heck of a lot better if *you* were with them," Dad grumbled. When he'd found out what had happened at tryouts over the summer, he'd been pretty steamed.

"Are you sure you can't arrest any of them for favoritism?" I asked.

"Hmmm, now that's a temptation. But this is a private club. Favoritism might be tacky, but strictly speaking, it isn't technically illegal."

Dad and I each lifted an end of the kayak and carried it, me walking forward, Dad walking backward. Over at the shore, Mrs. Wilcox and Mayor Franklin were drinking cups of coffee and chatting while they watched the Paddlers practice.

"Hi, Chief," Mrs. Wilcox said, after we'd checked in at the aquatic center. "You and Izzy seem to be coming here more than usual."

"We're training," Dad said. "Izzy's entered the regatta—she'll be racing one of my own pumpkins."

"Izzy entered the regatta?" Mayor Franklin asked, a strange edge to her voice.

"Yep," Dad said, slinging an arm around me. "She's going to be the first middle schooler to win it. You two and the Paddlers should come out to see her."

I haven't told Dad about my plan to convince Lauren I belonged on the Paddlers, but I'm pretty sure he's figured it out.

"That's right," I said. "I've gotten much faster since tryouts."

"You have?" Mrs. Wilcox asked, studying me.

"Loads faster," Dad said, smiling widely. "Anyways, we'll see you around."

"That was fun," he said in a low voice as he dragged the kayak into the water. "I thought Mayor Franklin was going to choke on her coffee. Too bad your mother wasn't here to see it."

Once I'd put on my life vest and some sunblock, I grabbed my paddle. I was ready to shove off—until Dad loaded up my kayak with the tote bags full of rocks.

"We need to add weight," he said, when I started to protest. "The kayak is sleek and smooth, but when you race Bozo, there will be more pounds to account for."

The rocks definitely added more weight, but I paddled as fast as I could, and surprisingly enough, I still made good time. I practiced for a couple hours, until Dad suggested we take a break for lunch.

We spread out a blanket and unpacked our lunches. The day was sunny and warm, and I dug my toes into the sand as I ate. "Autumn in Northern California," Dad said, stretching out and tipping his head back. "I love days like this."

I loved them too. But I'd love this particular one a whole lot more if Mom were here. "When did you say she was coming?" I asked.

Dad didn't have to ask who I meant. "Soon, Izzy."

We continued eating, and a man who worked at the olive oil shop near the Kaleidoscope came jogging by. When he saw us, he slowed down and removed his earbuds. "Hi, Chief. Any leads on catching the Star Bandit?"

"Sure," Dad answered. "Everyone at the station is working round the clock on it. New tips come in all the time."

They do? I put my sandwich down. All of a sudden, I didn't feel so hungry anymore.

"That's good to hear," he said, putting his buds back in. "Keep up the good work!"

After he'd jogged away I said, "Is that true, about all the tips?"

"Not even a little bit," Dad answered briskly. "But you can't actually *say* that. It's bad for morale." He shook his head. "That Star Bandit is a ghost."

"Do you think he's a bad person?" I asked, feeling a pit in my stomach.

"I don't know what to think. Maybe he's misguided— and maybe he's not a *he* at all. Maybe the Star Bandit is a girl. Maybe we shouldn't be so quick to give all the credit to a boy."

I glanced over at Dad to see if he was becoming suspicious, but he was just staring at the lake while he talked, an easygoing expression on his face.

"Credit?" I repeated.

Dad laughed. "Or blame, depending on how you look at it. I'm sure we'll catch him—or *her*, or *them*—soon."

"I'm sure you will," I said.

I promise, I added silently to myself.

After we were finished eating, Dad asked me to throw away our trash while he made a quick phone call. On the way back, I caught the tail end of his conversation:

"Janine, call me back. I'm serious—you need to get here this time and watch. Izzy's waiting."

I kept on waiting. We trained for a few more hours. I kept glancing over my shoulder, hoping I'd see Mom standing on the shore, watching me. We stayed longer than usual—long after my arms and legs were aching—until we finally decided to quit for the day and head home.

I'd like to say I was surprised Mom never showed up, but I wasn't.

In the truck, a sad silence stretched like a chilly shadow over me and Dad. "Your mother always wished she could sing," he said finally, as he turned the car into our neighborhood. "It must be pretty exciting for her, watching Carolyn get the lead as a freshman."

"I know." Grandma Bertie once told me that Mom tried out for the high school musical every year and every year she came home crying when the cast list was posted and her name wasn't on it. Then, ironically, she gave birth to a daughter who was a bona fide musical genius. I guessed it *was* pretty exciting for her. Carolyn, too, of course.

But not so much for me.

After Dad and I unloaded the truck, I headed inside and found Carolyn in the den, strumming her guitar. "How was rehearsal?" I asked, and my voice sounded strange.

Carolyn stopped strumming; her eyes went on high alert. "Fine. How was the lake?"

"Fine. Did you memorize your lines?"

"Not yet. Did you improve your time?"

We kept on that way, like our conversation was a ball we were tossing back and forth. Except we weren't talking about kayaking, or Carolyn's rehearsal. Sometimes you can be saying one thing, but actually talking about something totally different.

"Where's Mom?" I asked.

"She just left," Carolyn answered, still watching me

with careful eyes. "We were hungry, so she went to pick something up for dinner."

"That must be real nice, having someone at your beck and call all the time. Is she going to cut your meat and do your dishes for you too?"

"Izzy." Carolyn let out a long breath. "I *told* her she didn't have to stay, and that I could catch a ride home with someone else."

"I guess technically you could have," I said. "But that would imply you have a friend other than Layla."

I saw the hurt spreading across Carolyn's face, but I couldn't bring myself to apologize. Here's the thing we never talk about: There's a cost to being a musical genius. While Carolyn is at her lessons on the weekends, other girls her age are going to the movies, or the mall. They're becoming friends. Meanwhile, Carolyn is by herself, practicing. If it weren't for Layla, who Carolyn's been friends with since kindergarten, she might actually be friendless.

"That's not fair, Izzy. I didn't—"

"You have no idea what's fair," I said. "Everyone works around your schedule like you're the president of the universe, and you don't even realize it."

My mouth was like an angry puppy let off his leash:

full of energy and ready to make a mess out of everything. I knew if I stuck around I'd say all the nasty things I was thinking, so I ran upstairs and lay down on my bed. I stayed there for a while, long enough for the sky outside to turn thick and gloomy.

Two soft taps sounded at the door—Carolyn's signature knock.

"Go away!" I yelled, even though I knew I couldn't keep her out. It was *her* room, after all.

The door opened, and Carolyn padded across the room and slid into bed beside me.

"The mouth strikes again," I said, as she wrapped an arm around me. "I'm sorry."

"I know," she said. "I'm sorry too."

"For what? *You* didn't do anything."

Carolyn was quiet for a second. "I guess I'm sorry things aren't fair—I *do* realize it. I just don't know what to do about it." She rolled over to look at me. "Mom barely pays attention to me at the rehearsals. She's always trying to talk to the other moms."

"Yeah, but when she's talking to them, she's bragging about *you*, right?"

"Yeah . . . but I think she does it more for herself, not for me."

We lay there in silence, until Carolyn said, "Want to go spy on Grandma Bertie and Aunt Mildred? They're fighting over the TV remote again."

"I was thinking about going outside to hang out in the treehouse."

Carolyn smiled. "If you do, I'll open our window and play Beethoven, as loud as I can. After that I'll—Oh . . . Hi, Mom."

I looked over. Mom was standing in the doorway, glancing nervously between me and Carolyn. She held a bulging brown paper bag.

"I brought home Chando's," she said.

Chando's is a taco stand a few towns over. It's my favorite, but we hardly ever go there because it's an hour drive one way. Mom must have broken a bunch of speeding laws to be back already.

"Chando's," I said, sitting up. "Really, you bought me a taco?"

"Really—and not just one taco. A whole bag of them. I also stopped off and picked up some mint chocolate chip ice cream."

Mint chocolate chip, also my favorite.

Mom and I stared at each other. We were quiet, but our eyes were saying a lot.

"I thought we could eat in the den and watch a movie together." She paused, then added, "Is that okay?"

"Yeah, Mom," I said, pulling back the covers and standing up. "It's okay."

Like I said, sometimes you can be saying one thing but actually talking about something totally different.

25

THE CHARM GIRLS?

The opportunity to redeem myself arrived with Mrs. Whippie's fourth letter, on the afternoon the few remaining green leaves in town exploded into fiery shades of red, orange, and yellow. The next day, I went to school and found Daisy, Violet, and Sophia, and asked each of them to meet me at my house after school.

They all said they'd be there.

"Wow," Sophia said, as she pulled herself up through the hole in my treehouse floor and saw the star-stickered walls. "Is this the Charm Girls' secret hideout?"

"Charm what?" Violet asked.

"Charm Girls," Sophia answered as she settled herself on the floor. "I guess that's how I think of you guys. So what's up?"

"I know why you asked us to meet," Daisy said eagerly. "The next letter came, right?"

I nodded and held up the creamy envelope, which I'd already opened. I had told myself I wouldn't open it until the other girls arrived, but my hands aren't always the obeying kind. The envelope was extra chunky, so I figured Mrs. Whippie had included a bracelet for Daisy along with the charms for our new tasks.

I was right. When I opened the envelope and fished inside, there was Daisy's bracelet, along with a jukebox and a paint palette charm. Also inside were three pink cupcake charms.

"I love cupcakes!" Daisy said, after I showed everyone the envelope's contents. "I hope we get to eat a ton of them!"

"Don't get too excited," I said. "There's a little more to it than that."

"So if I help with this task I can get a bracelet the next time, right?" Sophia asked as Daisy put hers on.

I nodded. "I'll write to Mrs. Whippie and ask." I unfolded the letter and read it to everyone:

Dear Izzy,

I've sent along Daisy's bracelet and charms for the last task—please welcome her to my school. No, a prize unlike any other doesn't refer to cash. I'm talking about something much better than money, but you'll just have to wait and see what it is!

What's all this nonsense about odd vision and not fitting in? There are plenty worse things in this world than not fitting in—like fitting in way too much. You strike me as a real original, Izzy Malone, in a world that loves carbon copies. If you think you beautified something, I believe you. I've never understood why folks love safe, neutral colors so much. Colors are what make this world worth living in. If God wanted a world full of gray-loving, cranky sourpusses, he would have made us all like my grandmother!

Now, for your next task, I found out that the Dandelion Historical Society's dessert auction is coming up. I'd like you and your friends to bake a bunch of cupcakes and donate them. Then you all will have earned your charm, and you may place it on your bracelet. Write me a letter and let me know how it went.

"Mrs. Whippie's letters are extremely bamboozling," Violet said when I finished.

"Bam-*what*?" Sophia asked.

"Bamboozling," Daisy said. "That's Violet speak for . . . well, something. You'll get used to it." She scowled. "I hate baking. Can't we just buy a ton of cupcakes and donate them?"

"No," I said. "I want to bake them. As many as we possibly can. Then we'll put stickers on them and say they're from the Star Bandit."

Generally speaking, I hate baking too, or any kind of cooking, which Grandma Bertie says is a straight-up tragedy. But I knew not telling Mom and Dad I was the Star Bandit was as good as lying straight to their faces. I didn't want to be a liar. I wanted to tell Mom everything—but not before the Star Bandit did something nice to help the whole town and show everyone that he—that *I*—wasn't a nuisance, or a vandal.

"When is the auction?" Sophia asked.

"Friday night," Violet answered. "Ms. Harmer is on the planning committee, and I heard her tell Dad that since everyone's getting ready for Pumpkin Palooza the next day they're afraid they won't get enough donations. They probably could use some extra baked goods."

"How are we supposed to bake a ton of cupcakes and say it's from the Star Bandit without anyone knowing they actually came from us?" Daisy asked.

We were silent while we all thought about it. No one seemed to have any ideas. Violet stared out the window, and Daisy picked up Mrs. Whippie's envelope and tapped it against her knee.

"My mom is closing the shop on Friday and taking my brothers on an all-day field trip with their class, so they won't be back until after dinner," Sophia said. "I could get everything ready in the morning, and then as soon as we get out of school, we could start baking. I have a pumpkin pie cupcake recipe I really like."

"I have allowance money saved up," Violet said. "I could help buy the ingredients."

"Me too," Daisy said.

"Maybe we could meet at lunch tomorrow and you guys could give me the money so I can buy everything?" Sophia said.

Daisy, Violet, and I glanced at each other. "You mean, like in the cafeteria?" I asked.

"Yeah, why not?"

I had to admit, it didn't sound all that bad. It was getting pretty cold sitting out under my tree. "Okay," I said.

"But I don't want to sit behind the Paddlers like last time."

"I'm in," Daisy said.

"I'm in too," Violet said. She sniffed and added, "What's that smell?"

"Dinner," I answered. "My mom's working on her chili recipe again."

Something changed in Violet's eyes, and I wondered what this time of day was like for her, when the sky turned lavender and smelled like dinners cooking and parents coming home. It seemed to me that with Mrs. Barnaby gone and no siblings, it could be a lonely time for Violet.

"Do you want to stay for dinner?" I asked.

"Yes," she said immediately. "If you don't think it would be any trouble?"

"I'll stay," Daisy said. "Grandma and Grandpa and Delia are so busy getting ready for Pumpkin Palooza, I haven't had anything but microwave dinners for weeks."

"Can I stay too?" Sophia asked quietly.

One thing I like about Grandma Bertie, Aunt Mildred, and even Mom is that they will never turn away a hungry soul.

"Sure," I said, and pretty soon Daisy, Violet, and Sophia had their phones out and were texting their families.

As I watched them tap away, I thought about how

I always ate lunch under my tree. Violet ate outside the music room, Daisy ate in the *Grapevine* office, and Sophia ate in the cafeteria. Four different places, but I was pretty sure we had one thing in common: We all ate alone. I guess I wasn't the only one finding middle school life difficult.

Daisy, Violet, and Sophia put their phones away, and one by one we climbed down the ladder and headed inside, just as the sky was darkening and Big D and Orion were coming out to play. I didn't stop to chat, though. I was too busy leading us to the kitchen, where it was brimming with light, and with four empty bowls, just waiting to be filled.

CHAPTER 26

CRUSH DIBS!

The dessert auction was being held in Hollow Hall, a multipurpose room on Iris Street, which borders the east end of Dandelion Square. By the time Friday afternoon rolled around, we still hadn't figured out how to slip the Star Bandit cupcakes into the auction without anyone noticing. Since Daisy and I didn't like to bake, and Sophia and Violet did, Sophia told Daisy and I to figure out a plan while she and Violet worked on the cupcakes.

Daisy and I had spent the last couple hours sitting on some folding chairs at the back of the hall while we brainstormed, but so far, we had nothing.

"I am so disappointed in us," Daisy said. "We were so great at the dance, creating that distraction."

"Yeah," I said, "I don't see how we can come up with one this time."

All over the hall, people were scurrying around. Scooter McGee and a bunch of other men and women from the Rotary Club were setting up folding chairs in front of a raised stage where the auction would take place. Ms. Harmer and Mr. Barnaby were stringing orange twinkle lights across the ceiling. Mayor Franklin was directing a few high school boys and telling them where to set up tables to display the baked goods. Over at the check-in table, Stella and Lauren were receiving all incoming desserts in between the seemingly more important task of taking selfies with their cell phones.

"Maybe we could bypass the Bobblehead Twins and drop our cupcakes on a display table when no one's looking," Daisy said.

"Won't work," I said, shaking my head. "It's too open. Someone will see us put them there, and as soon as they notice the star stickers . . ."

Daisy sighed. "I hate to say it, but maybe we should pack it in and head over to Sophia's. Maybe together the four of us can come up with something."

We stood up to leave. I turned around to start for the exit—and smacked right into Austin, who was walking the opposite way.

"Ouch! Watch where you're—Oh . . . Hi, Izzy."

"Hey, Austin," I said, rubbing my shoulder. "How's it going?"

"Fine." Austin didn't say anything else, but he didn't move out of my way, either. He just kept jiggling from one foot to another, looking everywhere but at me. Things were still weird between us. There had been a couple nights when I was working out on the rowing machine and I heard him shooting hoops in his driveway, but he didn't invite me over.

"So," I said, pointing to the plastic container in his hand, "are you staying for the auction tonight?"

"No. But my mom wanted to donate loaves of her banana bread, so she made me drop some off."

"Oh. Cool," I said.

Daisy looked back and forth between the two of us and rolled her eyes.

"Anyways . . . I guess I should go," Austin said.

"Oh, okay. Bye," I said.

"Bye," Austin said.

"Weird," Daisy said after he'd left. "What's up with you and Captain Awkward?"

"Nothing. I—"

"Isabella?" came Mom's voice.

"Izzy," I said, turning around. Behind us, Mom was in full-blown Candidate Malone mode: a navy suit, bright red lipstick, and hair so stiff it didn't move, even though a breeze was blowing in from the open doors.

I figured it was just a matter of time before she showed up. With a little less than two weeks to the election, I knew she wanted to volunteer for every community event she possibly could.

"Grandma Bertie told me you were going over to a friend's house this afternoon?" Her cell phone beeped then, and she took it out of her purse to check it.

"I am. Daisy and I are headed there now."

"Hi, Mrs. Malone," Daisy said.

"That's fine," Mom said, looking up from her cell phone long enough to nod at Daisy, "but I'd like you back here in two hours. Grandma Bertie and the Knatterers have been baking all day, and they'll be arriving with a ton of muffins." She finished texting and dropped her phone back into her purse. "I'd like you to help them unload when they get here."

"That sounds great," Daisy said, with a meaningful look at her charm bracelet. "I can help too."

"Right," I said quickly. "We'd love to. In fact, I'll have Violet and our friend Sophia help also."

"Mission accomplished," Daisy whispered after Mom turned away.

We left Hollow Hall and turned from Iris onto Thistle Street, and continued walking until we came upon a sign that read CHARMING TRINKETS. Off the curlicue on the S hung a bracelet with colorful charms. A sign in the window said the shop was closed, but I rang the bell anyway. Sophia told me her family lived in the apartment upstairs.

"How cool is it to live right above Dandelion Square?" Daisy said while we waited. "If that's Sophia's window directly up there, she could see the town Christmas tree in December."

The door unlocked. "Hi!" Sophia said. She was sweaty, and her cheeks were streaked with flour. She held the door wide. "Come in and check out the shop."

The walls were painted pale pink. White display cases zigzagged around the room, except for a corner where two gray couches were pushed in front of a brick fireplace. Every available surface was covered in jewelry. Jangly bracelets, dangly earrings, chunky necklaces in every color you could imagine, rhinestone-studded handbags. Along the entire back wall were gold- and silver-chained bracelets, and tons of accompanying charms. A lipstick charm, a hamburger charm, a sparkly orange pumpkin charm. Charms of every letter of the alphabet. I even saw a treasure box and a paint palette charm. They looked like exact matches to the charms on my own bracelet.

"See what I mean?" Sophia said, following my gaze. "That's why I thought Mrs. Whippie must be buying her charms here." She motioned us over to a side room where her mom kept extra stock. At the back was a staircase, which led up to the apartment.

In the living room, Daisy stopped to pick up a photograph of a man in a fireman's uniform. "Is this your dad?" After Sophia nodded, Daisy asked, "Does he work at the Dandelion Hollow station?"

"My dad doesn't live with us," Sophia murmured, taking the photograph from Daisy and putting it back on the shelf. "My parents are separated."

"Sorry," Daisy said quickly. "My dad doesn't live with me either."

We followed Sophia, and the scent of cloves and nutmeg, into the kitchen, where there was a small table, and a window seat that—like Daisy had said—looked out on Dandelion Square. The island in the middle was covered with pumpkin pie cupcakes. Steam was still rising in sweet spirals from one batch. Violet, who was frosting a cupcake with a plastic spoon, looked up and said, "Isn't this great?"

"Wow," Daisy said. "How many did you guys make?"

"Sophia is a baking master," Violet said. "I've eaten six cupcakes, and they are spectacular!" She winced as her stomach made a weird sound. "Six may have been too many."

"It was nothing," Sophia said, flushing. "I baked a couple dozen last night, and Violet has been helping me with the rest. Did you guys figure out how to get them into the auction?"

"Yeah." I joined Violet and started frosting a cupcake, and told them about running into my mom. "We'll slip them in with the baked goods from the Knatterers."

"We also saw Austin Jackson," Daisy spoke up. "He was being a total spaz to Izzy."

"That's not surprising," Violet said. "Austin has a crush on Izzy."

"What?" I said. "No, he doesn't."

"Yes, he does," Violet said. "He's stuck up for you a few times when someone called you Toad Girl. And at the Harvest Dance, he asked me where you were. He wanted to ask you to dance."

"I know," I said. "But he only did that because Ms. Harmer made him."

When I looked up from my cupcake, Daisy, Violet, and Sophia were staring at me. "What?"

"Izzy," Sophia began, "a boy usually doesn't go out of his way to ask a girl to dance unless he likes her."

"Right." Violet nodded. "You should have seen the look on his face when Stella grabbed his hand and marched him off to the dance floor."

"Yesterday at lunch, he kept glancing over at our table," Daisy volunteered. She frowned. "At first I thought he just had a weird eye twitch, but now I think maybe he was looking at you."

"So the question is"—Sophia paused dramatically—"do you like him back?"

All three of them stared at me, but I didn't know what to say. Generally speaking, I didn't know how it worked with having friends and liking boys. Yesterday in science class, Macy Turner and Hannah Warren, who have been best friends since first grade and are usually fairly normal as far as people go, were about to kill each other over Ethan Stone, which I thought was the most ridiculous thing ever, since up until this year Ethan had a serious nose-picking habit.

See what I mean? Boy-crazy aliens, I'm telling you.

"Well," I said hesitantly. "If I *did* like him, and some-one else liked him . . . I wouldn't want it to be a problem."

"Please," Daisy said, rolling her eyes, "no one in this room likes Austin Jackson."

Violet concentrated on frosting her cupcake, and Sophia said, "Yeah, and even if we did, you can always call crush dibs."

"What's crush dibs?" I asked.

"It's something we did at my old school," Sophia answered. "If a girl decided she had a crush on a boy, she called crush dibs—then none of her friends were allowed to like him."

"That seems unfair," Violet said.

"It seems gross," Daisy said. She turned to me. "Do you really like Austin Jackson?"

"Well," I said, "if no one else does . . . then yes, I do. Crush dibs!" I yelled, and Sophia started laughing.

Daisy and Sophia picked up spoons and joined Violet and me at the island. We talked about school and fin-ished frosting the cupcakes. It was the best afternoon I'd ever had.

CHAPTER 27

FOURTH TIME'S THE CHARM

We bundled up the cupcakes in plastic wrap—smearing the frosting, unfortunately—stuck some star stickers on top, and placed them in Sophia's mom's old baking tins. That way no one would know they came from the Star Bandit until they lifted the lid—by which point the four of us planned to be safely in the audience, politely watching the auction.

By the time Grandma Bertie's minivan pulled up in front of Hollow Hall, the old-fashioned lampposts that dotted Dandelion Square had flickered on, and Daisy, Violet, Sophia, and I were waiting at the curb, each of us carrying a paper grocery bag with tins inside.

"Hi, dear," Grandma Bertie said as she got out of the car. "The muffins are in the back. It's so nice of you girls to help out a couple old birds like us. You really didn't need to."

"Speak for yourself, Bertha," Aunt Mildred said as she slammed the passenger door shut. "I've about had it up to here with all this muffin nonsense. If Izzy and her friends want to take it from here, they're welcome to it."

"No problem, Aunt Mildred, we've got this," I said. "Step away from the vehicle. A major muffin operation is about to commence."

Violet, Daisy, and Sophia crowded around me, forming a shield, while I started emptying the grocery bags and placing the tins in the canvas bags full of the Knatterers' muffins.

"You'll have to unpack the bags and put the tins at the bottom, or they'll squash the muffins," Violet whispered.

"That'll take too long," I said, although I could see Violet was right.

"We've got time," Violet said.

She was right again, because Grandma Bertie and Aunt Mildred were fighting.

"I don't see why you always have to be such a royal pain in the you-know-what," Grandma Bertie was saying.

"*I'm* a pain?" Aunt Mildred snorted. "You and your Knatterers spent the entire day gossiping and sipping your coffee while *I* baked those muffins."

"You've never baked a day in your life."

"Correction: I've baked exactly one day in my life, and today was it. No thanks to you and your lazy friends."

While they argued, I quickly unpacked the canvas bags, placed our tins at the bottom, and started repacking the bags. As I worked, I could feel my heart filling with hope. It was the fourth task, and with the four of us working together, I hoped that tonight would be fourth time's the charm, and that I could show everyone the Star Bandit was actually a do-gooder. A sloppy one, maybe, but a do-gooder, nevertheless.

"Hello, Milly!" came Scooter McGee's voice behind us. "Fancy seeing you here tonight."

"Fancy nothing. I told you at the Kaleidoscope yesterday: Bertha roped me into helping out."

"It's delightful all the same," Scooter said as I repacked the last bag. "Janine's here. She told me you're helping out with her booth tomorrow at Pumpkin Palooza."

"It appears I'm becoming a regular upstanding citizen." From the tone of Aunt Mildred's voice, it didn't sound like she thought much of upstanding citizens.

"Finished," I whispered to Daisy, Violet, and Sophia. The four of us started removing the bags from the minivan.

"Janine is lucky to have you," Scooter said. "As you may know, I'll be there as well. I'm emceeing the regatta later in the afternoon, and I was wondering if you would care to join me for lunch."

"I can't stand carnival food. It gives me indigestion."

"Dear," Grandma Bertie said loudly to Aunt Mildred, "when a nice man asks to pay for your lunch, the polite thing to do is say yes."

"I know that!" Aunt Mildred glared at Grandma Bertie, who merely smiled and batted her eyelashes. She turned back to Scooter. "Fine—We may dine together. But if you think I consider hot dogs and cotton candy a proper meal, you've got another thing coming." Aunt Mildred turned away from a smiling Scooter and began marching toward the hall, calling over her shoulder, "Girls! Are you planting roots over there? Get moving with those bags!"

The auction was about to begin, and Hollow Hall was nearly filled. Grandpa and Grandma Caulfield were sitting in the back row. A dark-haired woman who I recognized from the pictures in Sophia's house as her mom sat a few rows ahead of them. Two twin boys sat next to her, and they waved to Sophia when they saw her. Mr. Barnaby and Ms. Harmer were up on the stage, fiddling with the microphone. Mayor Franklin had joined Stella and Lauren at the check-in counter, and her eyes widened when she saw us all marching toward her.

"Good Lord, Bertha," she said to Grandma Bertie. "Those are a lot of bags. What are you donating tonight?"

"Chocolate chip muffins!" Grandma Bertie said. "Courtesy of Janine Malone's campaign!"

Mayor Franklin's eyes went flat. "Wonderful," she said.

While we placed the bags on the table, Lauren looked at me and said, "My mom told me you're racing in the pumpkin regatta tomorrow."

My heart began to beat faster. "I am. I think I can win, too. I'm a pretty fast paddler." Next to Lauren, Stella looked like she was slowly filling up with steam.

"I've been thinking," Lauren continued, "maybe we were too hasty in making our decision over the summer. Maybe the Paddlers do need someone like you"— her eyes briefly flicked down to my tie-dye skirt, and she frowned—"or someone with your skills, anyway." She gave a sideways glance at Stella. "Some of us haven't been making enough of an effort lately. So maybe I'll come see the race tomorrow—consider it a second tryout."

"Awesome," I said, smiling widely as Stella shot a murderous look my way. "I'll see you tomorrow."

Lauren stood up and left. Meanwhile, at the other end of the table, Aunt Mildred suddenly raised her voice. "I'm telling you, we don't know how those got in there."

"They were in your bags. You mean to tell me you've never seen these before?" Mayor Franklin held up one of our tins and removed a plastic-wrapped bunch of cupcakes, the star stickers stuck to the top.

No, no, no! They weren't supposed to be discovered until the auction was already under way! I had been so busy talking to Lauren I hadn't realized Mayor Franklin had taken it upon herself to thoroughly inspect the contents of each bag, while Daisy, Sophia, and Violet were standing by with horrified looks, helpless to do anything.

"That's exactly what I'm telling you, Mrs. Franklin." Aunt Mildred's gaze briefly flickered over to me before she muttered something under her breath. I was pretty sure it was nasty French words.

"That's *Mayor* Franklin."

"What's going on?" Mom said, striding up to the table. "Why are you yelling at my aunt and my mother?"

"Because they delivered baked goods with star stickers on them. See?" Mayor Franklin handed Mom a tin.

"Those are exactly the kind of stickers the Star Bandit uses."

Mom laughed. "Are you telling me you think one of them is the Star Bandit? Don't be ridiculous. You've been working too hard, Kendra. I think you need to take a break."

Mom laughed again, until Stella said, "It's not that ridiculous, Mrs. Malone. After all, the Star Bandit *is* someone from your family. It's just not your aunt." She paused and shot me an evil grin. "It's Izzy."

"*What?*" Mayor Franklin said.

"Ridiculous," Grandma Bertie said.

"Crap," Daisy said.

"Language!" Mom snapped. She turned to Mayor Franklin. "I do not appreciate your daughter making false accusations about my daughter. You can say whatever you'd like about me during this election, but my daughter is off-limits."

"My daughter is not in the business of making false accusations," Mayor Franklin said. "Stella, what are you talking about?"

"It's true, Mrs. Malone. Honest," Stella said, in the kiss-butt voice she reserved for adults. "I mean, I guess I don't know for sure, but I saw Izzy the night Ms. Zubov's garden was vandalized. She was hanging around the play-ground over on the village green, and she had star stickers with her. They were glowing in the dark, and I could see her face. Remember, Mom, we had to pick something up from the olive oil store that night?"

"That's true," Mayor Franklin said, surprise crossing her face as she remembered. "Why, that must have been right before the vandalism happened."

"It wasn't vandalism," I blurted out.

"Izzy, *hush*." Violet nudged me in the shoulder, but it was too late. Mom suddenly got quiet and stared at me searchingly. "Is this true, Isabella?" she asked.

I had planned on telling her the truth, maybe even tonight. But not like this. Not with Mayor Franklin and Stella watching, both of them not quite hiding their glee.

"It's true," I said, and it felt like I was swallowing a mouthful of nails. "I'm the Star Bandit."

"You're the Star Bandit," Mom repeated woodenly. "The one who vandalized the wall—"

"I didn't vandalize anything."

"—and the one who ruined my campaign materials?"

"*That* was a complete accident."

"Accident?" Mom said, her voice rising. "I am so tired

of your excuses. We give you chance after chance, and you keep misbehaving."

"Mom you have to listen to me, please," I said, feeling panicky. "I never meant to—"

"You never *mean* to, Isabella. You just do."

"Janine," Grandma Bertie began, glancing around the room, "maybe we should—"

"Stay out of this, Mother." Mom turned back to me, fury swirling in her eyes. "Do you know how embarrassing this will be when everyone finds out? People will wonder, if I can't manage my own daughter, how can I possibly manage the whole town? Why do you have to make everything so difficult all the time? Why can't you be more like your sister and . . ."

She cut herself off abruptly, but her words hung in the air. They smelled like failure. My failure, for not being as talented or as easy to get along with as Carolyn. For always being a loudmouthed rough edge, when what Mom really wanted was a mild-mannered smooth surface.

"I'm not Carolyn," I said quietly. "I'm me. Not Carolyn, and not the sweet daughter Isabella you keep hoping I will be, but *me*, Izzy. And I'm tired of feeling bad about that." I paused and added, "I saw your campaign mailer, with the picture of you, Dad, and Carolyn—the one you didn't bother to include me in. I saw it on Ms. Zubov's porch, and I accidentally left the box open, and the wind blew them out of the box—but I never purposely tried to damage anything."

I couldn't take any more. Not Mom's sad expression, not Stella and Mayor Franklin's smug smiles, not the pity I saw in Aunt Mildred's and Grandma Bertie's eyes.

I turned and ran from the hall, the sound of Daisy, Violet, and Sophia's voices calling my name fading behind me like choir bells.

BRIGHT LIGHTS ON A DARK NIGHT

I ran out to Dandelion Square and through the village green, crunching across a carpet of golden leaves. It was just past dusk; the sky was sapphire blue and edged with an autumn chill. I stopped running when I reached the playground at the other end of the square, which was empty except for a couple high schoolers sucking face on the two swings. I sat down on the merry-go-round and stared at them, wishing I could sit on the swings.

Sticks and stones may break my bones, but words can never hurt me, I said to myself, and then waited to see if I felt any better.

I didn't.

Why can't you be more like your sister? Mom's words were sharp like knives, and they cut deep. I always knew she felt like she'd won the kid lottery with Carolyn and not so much with me, but it hurt to hear her actually say it, and I wished she didn't have to feel so embarrassed about being my mother.

I must have been staring at the high schoolers for a long time, because the girl came up for air long enough to say, "Take a picture, it'll last longer."

"Okay, if you insist," I said, pretending to remove a cell phone from my pocket. "But I think I'll take a video instead. You know, in case I need any pointers later. I never knew kissing could be so loud."

That sent them both stomping away indignantly, muttering about middle school pests, but I didn't feel like getting up to sit on the swings anymore, so I lay back on the merry-go-round and stared up at the sky. Clouds were rolling in, but I could still see Orion and Big D, and I began to tell them what had happened.

I wished I could lasso both of them and take them to Pumpkin Palooza tomorrow and to school next week, where everyone was sure to know I, Izzy Malone, Toad Girl, was the Star Bandit. Maybe their brilliance could save me from all the stares I was sure to get.

"I really wish just once you guys would answer me back," I said.

"Izzy? Who are you talking to?"

I was halfway out of my seat before Violet materialized out of the darkness. Daisy and Sophia were right behind her. Violet looked around. "Is someone else here?"

"No," I said. "I was just talking to the stars."

"Oh, okay," Violet said, like that was perfectly normal. She sat down on the merry-go-round. So did Daisy and Sophia. "We've been looking everywhere for you," she said. When I didn't answer, she added, "Did you know that after the sun, the closest star in our galaxy is Alpha Centauri? It's over four light-years away from Earth. It's actually not even just one star, but three of them, bound closely together."

"That's great, Violet," I said, lying back on the merry-go-round. "That's just what I need right now: an astronomy lesson."

"I guess what I'm saying is, those stars are trillions of miles away. But the three of us are right here. Why don't you talk to us instead?"

"There's nothing to talk about. You guys heard everything my mom said."

"I'm sure she didn't mean it," Sophia said. "She was just mad."

"That's what she'll tell me tomorrow. She'll say she just lost her temper. But the thing is, a part of her *did* mean it. I know she did."

Everyone was silent. One by one, I could hear them leaning back on the merry-go-round, till we were all four looking up. The clouds were still slowly drifting in, like white wispy fingers stretching across the night sky, but so far the stars were still visible and they glittered like diamonds.

"You know you're going to have to go back to the auction, right?" Violet said after a while.

"Yeah, but not right now."

"Not right now," Violet agreed.

"But when you do," Sophia said, "we'll be with you."

"And we will personally punch the lights out of anyone who messes with you," Daisy said.

"Daisy," Violet warned. "I don't think—"

"I'm just speaking allegorically, of course. Or maybe metaphorically? Or some other 'ally' word that only Violet knows," Daisy said, and everyone laughed.

After we quieted down, Sophia said, "Look at that view. The stars are beautiful."

"They sure are," I said. I couldn't help but wonder if Orion and Big D had somehow sent me Daisy, Violet, and Sophia.

Because maybe the best kind of friends are like stars: bright and beautiful, appearing in the darkness just when you need them, giving you a little bit of light on a dark night.

CHAPTER
29

PUMPKIN PIE PUKE

Next to me, I could feel Daisy getting restless. First she started jiggling her leg. Then she dug her heel into the sand and pushed off, so we slowly started to spin. I joined in, and soon the merry-go-round was whirling.

"Who's doing that?" Sophia asked.

"Izzy and Daisy," Violet answered. "And if you don't stop it I'm going to spew pumpkin pie puke all over you both."

"As your appointed escort," came a voice from the darkness, "I'm afraid vomit of any flavor is strictly prohibited."

Sophia and Violet screamed. Daisy jumped off the merry-go-round. I sat up and looked around. Scooter McGee stood by the swings, grinning.

"Mildred sent me to corral you girls," he said, coming closer. "It appears Izzy's father wishes to speak with her."

"I'll bet he does," I said, lying back down. "I am so dead. You guys might as well just say good-bye to me now."

"I don't think that will be necessary," Scooter said. "The Star Bandit's cupcakes saved the day. Or the night, I should say."

"What?" I sat back up. "What do you mean?"

"You girls ran away so fast, you didn't get to see the auction. Your cupcakes started a bidding war. Everyone wanted a piece of the Star Bandit's story." Scooter's eyes twinkled in the moonlight. "I myself paid five hundred dollars for a dozen cupcakes. Pumpkin pie, I believe." He glanced at Violet and frowned. "I do hope they don't cause serious indigestion."

"Just don't eat six of them and then go spinning on a merry-go-round," Violet said, clutching her stomach.

"You paid five hundred dollars?" Sophia said, sounding awed. "Are you serious?"

"Quite so," Scooter replied. "It's not often I get home-made cupcakes, especially ones from a notorious Dandelion Hollowian." He offered me his arm. "Well, Izzy Malone? Are you ready to 'face the music,' as they say?"

I stood up and took his arm. "I guess so," I said, and we left the playground, with Daisy, Violet, and Sophia following along behind us.

The walk back was way too quick. The display tables were empty, and the Rotary Club members were packing away the folding chairs. The hall was nearly deserted, except for Dad, who was waiting for us, along with Grandpa and Grandma Caulfield, Mr. Barnaby, and Mrs. Ramos. They were all standing in a circle chatting, while Sophia's brothers played on the floor with toy cars. Grandma Caulfield was the first to notice us, and her eyes narrowed as she said something to Dad, who turned to meet us.

"Great," Daisy muttered. "Looks like we're all doomed. Where is Delia when I really need her?"

"Where's Mom?" I asked Dad.

"Grandma Bertie and Aunt Mildred drove her home," he answered. "She wasn't feeling well."

"I'll excuse myself now and help with cleanup," Scooter said. "Holler if you need anything, Robert."

Dad nodded. "Thanks, Scooter." To me, he said, "Now, listen. I don't know—"

"Chief Malone?" Sophia stepped forward. "I just want you to know that if Izzy is in trouble, then I should be too. I knew she was the Star Bandit, and I helped her tonight.

I baked most of those cupcakes." She paused and glanced nervously at her mother. "I guess I'm sort of the Star Bandit too."

"Me too," Violet said. She looked at her dad and shrugged. "I helped clean Ms. Zubov's garden."

"Um . . . me three," Daisy said. "I helped Izzy get away so she could paint the wall at the dance. I'm also the Star Bandit."

"In a way, sir," Sophia said, "I guess you could say we're all the Star Bandit."

At that, all the parents began murmuring to each other, but I stayed quiet. It felt like something was lodged deep in my throat. I wasn't used to anyone sticking up for me. Usually, if I got into trouble, the kids at school were real quick to rat me out.

Something soft flashed in Dad's eyes. Then he went into Chief Malone mode and gestured to some folding chairs and ordered us to sit down. "Explain," he said, after we were settled.

"It all started with Mrs. Whippie's first letter," I said. "Remember that charm school you signed me up for?" I spent the next half hour telling Dad all about the letters and tasks, with Daisy, Violet, and Sophia occasionally jumping in.

"So . . . all this was to earn the charms on your brace-let?" he asked when we finished.

"Yes." I swallowed. "You believe me, don't you? I never tried to hurt Mom's campaign. I was going to tell you guys, I swear, after we auctioned off the cupcakes. I just wanted to do something right before I told you."

"I believe you, Izzy," Dad said. He glanced over at the other parents, who had been quietly listening all this time, and added, "I believe all *four* of you. But, Izzy—I think a long talk with your mother is in order."

I nodded. "I know."

"Does this mean you won't be arresting us, Chief Malone?" Daisy asked, shooting a quick look at her grand-parents. "Because if you are, I'd like to make my phone call, and call Delia."

Dad looked like he was trying not to smile. "I won't be arresting anyone tonight, Daisy. *But*," he added, his voice growing stern, "that does not mean the four of you aren't in *a lot* of trouble. As for *you*, Izzy, early next week you will go down to Principal Chilton's office. You will apologize for painting that wall and you will accept whatever consequences he gives you. You will also apol-ogize to Ms. Zubov for scaring the daylights out of her. And you're going to offer to clear out her garden at the end of the fall season. During the daytime, when she is not inclined to employ the services of her Taser. You will also be grounded for a month. And you can still help me get Bozo to Pumpkin Palooza tomorrow morning, and you can still race in the regatta in the afternoon, but that's about as much of the harvest festival as you're going to experience this year. The rest of your day will be spent helping out at your mother's booth. No rides, no games, no nothing. And . . . you will apologize to your mother. Do I make myself clear?"

"I promise," I said, nodding. "I will never get in this much trouble again."

"You had better mean that, Isabella."

"Iz—" I started to argue, until Violet clapped a hand over my mouth.

"That sounds great, Mr. Malone," she said.

We all went our separate ways after that. Daisy, Violet, and Sophia each went home with her family. Dad and I stuck around so we could help finish cleaning up. Just as Dad went to put the last of the folding chairs away, Scooter stopped to talk to me. "I overheard a little of what you said to your dad. Did you say 'Whippie' was the name of your school? That name sure brings back memories."

"Memories?" I said. "What do you mean?"

"I went to school with a Whippie once. Jack Whippie. So did your grandma and great-aunt, as a matter of fact." He shook his head sadly. "That was a real tragedy. Mildred loved him dearly," he said, and something fluttered at the edges of my memory. "If Jack hadn't died, I'll bet she would have married him."

My heart began to beat fast. I'd never heard of Jack Whippie, but if she had married him, that would have made her Mildred Whippie. *Mrs.* Mildred Whippie.

Could it be?

I pulled Mrs. Whippie's latest letter from my skirt pocket and flipped the envelope over so I could examine the postmark, which I never really noticed.

It read: Dandelion Hollow, California.

30

WILL THE REAL MRS. WHIPPIE PLEASE STAND UP?

Dandelion Hollow. *Not San Francisco.*

How was that possible? I always mailed my letters to the PO Box Mrs. Whippie gave me. But if the postmark said Dandelion Hollow, that would have to mean Mrs. Whippie mailed her letters from town.

As Dad and I silently drove home from the auction, I hooked the cupcake charm on my bracelet and remembered something I'd overheard not too long ago:

"We all miss someone."

"Oh, Milly, I know. I know we do."

"It looks like Mom's light is out," Dad said when we got home. "Maybe you could talk to her tomorrow."

"Sure, Dad," I said as I headed slowly up the staircase. "Tomorrow."

In the gap underneath Aunt Mildred's closed door a small strip of light spilled into the hallway. I knocked.

"Come in," Aunt Mildred said.

I opened the door and stepped inside. Aunt Mildred was sitting at a wooden desk, brushing her hair.

"Izzy, I am so glad you came to visit. . . ." She stopped abruptly when she saw the letter in my hand.

I looked around. My old room looked really different now. Cream-colored curtains framed the window. Teacups and porcelain jewelry boxes decorated the bookshelves and dresser. Colorful scarves were tacked to the walls. A pale pink throw rug was draped across a small couch.

And in the air hung the scent of roses and cream.

"Your room smells like my letters," I said. Aunt Mildred opened her mouth to speak, but I rushed on, "I heard something interesting a while back. I heard you and Grandma Bertie talking about someone you missed." I held up my wrist, and shook it, and the charms on my bracelet clinked together. "You were talking about Jack Whippie, weren't you?"

Aunt Mildred put down her hairbrush and stood up. "I wondered when you'd figure that out."

"*You're* Mrs. Whippie? You run the charm school?"

"There is no charm school . . . Not for anyone else but you and your friends, anyway."

"I don't understand," I said. "Do Mom and Dad know about this?"

"No." She gestured to the couch. "Come and sit . . . *Now*," she added, in her usual cranky tone, when I didn't move right away. "I'll tell you everything, but it'll take a while."

"I heard your parents talking one day about doing something unusual to get you to change your behavior," she began after we had both settled on the couch. "Janine mentioned a charm school, which, if you ask me, was a load of horse rubbish. I didn't think you'd appreciate some prissy-fissy school telling you how to hold a teacup or how to make polite conversation. What's the point in all *that* nonsense? You may not believe me, Izzy, but you remind me a lot of me when I was your age. You think it's hard being compared to Carolyn? Try having a twin sister who can charm the pants—excuse the expression—off of everything and everyone. Anyways, I saw how things were going for you, and I guess I thought maybe I could help somehow. After I saw that new store—Charming Trinkets—I came up with the idea for a different kind of

charm school. I made up a flier and put it in the mailbox—
your Mom was too busy to look too much into it, and I
used my old PO Box from San Francisco. I had your letters
forwarded from there back to Dandelion Hollow."

"But why did you use a bracelet and charms?" I asked.
"That's kind of odd."

In answer, Aunt Mildred reached over and picked
up a pink-and-white porcelain box from the dresser and
handed it to me. "Open it," she said.

"But—"

"Just open it. Trust me."

I lifted the lid. Inside was a charm bracelet, but it was
unlike any I'd ever seen. A gold chain, vintage-looking,
hosting more charms than I'd ever seen on one bracelet.
A tiny passport, an ice skate, a small book, an apple, a tea-
pot, a watering can, a miniature Eiffel Tower.

I looked up. "I don't understand."

"Jack Whippie was my high school beau—it's an
old-fashioned word, it means boyfriend. He asked me to
marry him, and I said yes." Aunt Mildred stared distantly
at the scarf on the wall, lost, I think, in a different time.
"We married in secret, on my eighteenth birthday, at the
courthouse. I didn't think my parents would approve—
Jack wasn't from a respectable family. That's one of my

greatest regrets: that I didn't even tell your grandma about it. She wasn't there to stand next to me on my wedding day.

"Jack didn't have money for diamonds, so instead of a ring, he gave me this charm bracelet. Of course, at the time, it was just a chain with a tiny book charm. He said that our life together was going to be like the best stories: adventurous and full of daring. He said every new place we traveled to, every new thing we did, we'd add a charm to my bracelet. I wish you could have seen him, Izzy," she said, and her voice cracked. "How young and handsome he looked that day." She took a deep breath. "Anyway, after the ceremony, we went our separate ways. Jack was going to tell his parents; I was going to tell mine—we thought it was best that way. Jack left right away—he wanted to drive me home, but I chose to walk instead. I knew what a fight I was gonna have with my parents, and I wanted to enjoy the spring rain."

Aunt Mildred winced, and her eyes became glassy. "Less than a block from the courthouse, a car ran a red light, right as Jack was driving through the intersection. In my nightmares, sometimes I still hear the sounds of screeching tires and shattering glass." She looked down. "Jack was killed instantly—the doctors said he probably never knew what hit him. I was in shock after that. I don't remember a lot from those days, but right after the funeral the county clerk pulled me aside and asked me if I wanted him to tear up our marriage license. He hadn't filed it yet—but he knew my parents, and under the circumstances, he thought it was better that way. I was an eighteen-year-old widow with no one to talk to, so I said yes."

She blinked, and a tear ran down her cheek. "No one ever knew that for less than one hour, Jack Whippie was my husband, not my boyfriend. I finally told your grandma one night, when I couldn't stop crying. I showed her my bracelet and told her everything. She knew I didn't like small-town life, and she told me I should still do it all, everything Jack and I had talked about, just on my own. 'Go out and earn those charms,' she said.

"A week later, she showed me an advertisement in the newspaper. They were looking for Americans to teach English in Europe. You didn't need any experience. You just needed a high school diploma and a willingness to travel. I had both, and by then I knew I needed to leave. So I did. First to San Francisco to get some training, then to France. On my first weekend in Paris, I set out to find a jewelry shop to purchase my first charm." She tapped the miniature Eiffel Tower on her bracelet. "After that, I was hooked. Every new thing I did, every new place I traveled, I bought a charm—I have so many now I can't even keep them all on the chain."

"But time passed, and I began to miss Bertie. Nearly forty years of traveling, and I knew it was time to come home. I guess when I saw what your grandma has—a lovely family—it made me remember again what I lost when Jack died, and I've been pretty bitter about it. Your parents are saints for putting up with me."

She looked at me and sighed. "Writing those letters gave me a chance to be someone else for a while, instead of cranky old Aunt Mildred." She smiled mischievously. "And I can't say it hasn't been a laugh, watching everyone in town get so worked up over the Star Bandit—when she's been right here the whole time."

"You knew?" I said.

Aunt Mildred rolled her eyes. "You sent your letters to *me*, remember? I may be old, but I'm not brain-dead." She patted my wrist. "The memories and the friends you make, Izzy, *that's* a prize unlike any other, because they're yours alone. It's your life, your story, and no one else's."

I stared at my own bracelet—at the tiny jukebox, paint palette, cupcake, envelope, and treasure box—and wondered what my story would look like, if I kept adding to it, charm by charm. When I was as old as Aunt Mildred, would I care that some rotten kids at school used to call me Toad Girl? I bet I wouldn't—but maybe one day I'd buy myself a tiny toad charm, because I wouldn't want to forget it either. Maybe I'd even buy a star charm, to remind myself that once upon a time I was the Star Bandit, and for a short time, the whole town was talking about me.

Aunt Mildred held out her bracelet. "This is the most valuable thing I own. It represents the life I've lived these last forty years. But it's too heavy for my wrist now; I haven't put any charms on it in a long time. I suppose I'm too old for adventures, and since I don't have any children of my own, well . . . I'd like you to have it. I'd planned to give it to you after your last task, but I guess now is as good a time as any."

I looked at the bracelet, all golden and colorful; it was making a musical, tinkling sound as the charms clinked together in Aunt Mildred's trembling hands.

But if the bracelet was the story of her life, it seemed wrong for me to take it. After all, her story wasn't over yet. Aunt Mildred was still alive.

"I don't think you're too old for adventures, Aunt Mildred. I think you should keep it."

"Maybe," she said doubtfully. She settled the bracelet back in the porcelain box and stood up. "I have something else for you." She removed a tiny silver box from her desk and handed it to me.

Inside the box, a small butterfly charm rested on pale pink velvet. The wings were golden and plated with shiny blue and green abalone shell and speckled with tiny rhinestones.

"Wow, Aunt Mildred. Of all the charms you've given me, I think this is the prettiest. What do I need to do to earn it?"

Aunt Mildred shook her head. "Nothing. This one is to help you remember."

"Remember what?"

"The butterfly is one of God's most beautiful creatures. But for the first half of its life, that butterfly inches along as a clunky caterpillar, moving slower than all the others, never knowing that one day, things will change. *They* will change. I know starting middle school hasn't been easy, but you just keep being yourself and making memories—building a good story—and one day you're gonna wake up and realize you've changed, and instead of inching along, you've sprouted wings, and you're flying, soaring higher than you ever thought you could."

She ran her finger over the tiny golden wings and continued, "I know Janine said some terrible things tonight, but I'll tell you something right now: Just because your mother has trouble fitting into her own skin doesn't mean you need to feel uncomfortable in yours. Things will change in that department too. You may not believe this, but your mother used to drive Bertha crazy. In the letters your grandma wrote me, it was always full of the things Janine did to irritate her. But one day the two of them woke up and realized they loved each other to pieces, and they weren't strangers anymore. I believe that will happen for you and your mom too someday. Until then, you're just going to have to be patient and accept her as she is."

"But I'm not the patient kind," I argued. "Generally speaking, me and patience aren't on speaking terms."

"Well, Lord in heaven, Izzy," Aunt Mildred said, rolling her eyes again, "none of the spunky ones ever are. But what *other* choice do we have?"

CHAPTER
31
LUNCH?

"Wake up, sleepyhead! Or should I say: Wake up, sleepy Star Bandit!"

I rolled over in bed and blinked at Carolyn, who was already dressed for the day. "Five minutes," I said, and closed my eyes.

"Nope, not in five minutes. *Now*. Dad says he and Bozo are pulling out of here in an hour, so you might want to get your lazy behind out of bed sometime this century."

Carolyn began to sing at the top of her lungs—some song in Italian she knows I hate—and I couldn't drown her out, not even when I buried my head under my pillow.

Most days, I think my sister is amazing. But times like

these, when she takes it upon herself to become my own personal operatic alarm clock, I wish I had a roll of duct tape to shut her up. I settled for throwing my teddy bear at her.

"Missed!" she said, and kept singing.

"All right, all right. Zip it." I sat up. "I need to talk to Mom anyways before we all leave."

"Um . . ." Carolyn's eyes shifted away, and I could tell she knew all about our big fight last night. "She already left."

"She *left*?"

"Yeah." Carolyn nodded apologetically. "She said she wanted to be the first to set up her booth, so she, Grandma Bertie, and Aunt Mildred left an hour ago."

"Oh." I lay back down. I'd figured after such a terrible fight last night she'd want to make up, or punish me, or *talk* to me, at least. But Pumpkin Palooza was a pretty big day for her campaign; I guess she didn't want to waste any of it.

"So . . . you know I'm the Star Bandit?" I asked, staring up at the ceiling.

Carolyn nodded. "Impressive. You are a not-so-evil genius, and I love it."

"Sure. But you know what everyone's going to be

saying today: *Gosh that odd Izzy Malone. I knew there was something not quite right about her. She's nothing like her sister, Carolyn.*"

We were silent until Carolyn took off her jacket and said, "Move over." She stretched out on the bed next to me. "Mom didn't mean it," she said softly.

"She meant it a little bit." We stared at the ceiling together until I said, "Do you know how much easier my life would be if you weren't so wonderful all the time?"

Carolyn thought about that for a second. "Would your life be easier if I was a juvenile delinquent?"

"Yes. Yes, it would," I said. "Can you get on that?"

"Sure—I'll add it to my to-do list. In fact, I think I have an opening after my guitar lesson today. Become a juvenile delinquent, check." She paused, and added, "People think I'm odd too, you know. I told some girls at school that I practiced on the piano two hours every morning and they looked at me like I was the biggest dork they'd ever seen."

I laughed. "Did you tell them *how* you practice?"

Every morning at precisely five a.m., Carolyn wakes up, sticks in her earbuds, and cranks her iPod with classical music. Then she places her fingers one inch above the piano and plays silently, her fingers never actually touching the keys, so she won't wake up anyone in the house.

"Hey." Carolyn pointed up at a pattern on the ceiling. "I think I see Italy."

"That's not Italy. That's a boot."

"Duh. Have you ever even looked at a map of Europe? That's exactly what Italy looks like." She sat up. "I have to get going, but I'll head over to the festival after my lessons are over." She smiled. "I can't wait to watch you race."

After I got ready for the day I went out to the backyard. Austin and Mr. Jackson were already there with Dad, who was holding a tape measure and smiling proudly. Bozo was officially the biggest pumpkin he'd ever grown. Dad had to rent a forklift to get him onto Mr. Jackson's huge flatbed truck.

I felt weird that Austin had been standing in my backyard while I changed and brushed my teeth, so I ignored him and turned to talk to his dad.

"Hi, Mr. Jackson."

"Hello, Izzy. Are you ready for the regatta?"

"Absolutely, sir. I've been working out on Dad's rowing machine every day."

"Have you ever raced a giant pumpkin before?"

"No, but there's a first time for everything."

Mr. Jackson grinned. "I suppose there is. Just promise me you'll beat Mike Harrison."

"Amen to that," Dad said. "Every single time I walk into the hardware store, he goes on and on and *on*. . . ."

Once the truck was loaded up and ready to go, Dad drove it slowly through town with Mr. Jackson riding in the passenger seat, while Austin and I waved from either side of Bozo in the back. The day was overcast and brisk—scarf and caramel apple cider weather—and the sidewalks were filled with people on their way to Pumpkin Palooza. Men doffed their hats, and children riding on their father's shoulders waved as we passed them.

Pumpkins, pimply squashes, and scarecrows on hay bales lined the long driveway up to Caulfield Farm. A special staging area had been set up for everyone participating in the regatta. Dad stopped at a line of trucks—each of them with a large pumpkin in the back—and shut off the car. At the front of the line sat a forklift and a gigantic scale. Each pumpkin had to be weighed before it could be hollowed out and turned into a boat. The trick was to grow a pumpkin large enough you could sit in, but not so huge it would be too clunky to row.

Daisy was standing in front of the scale, writing down

the name and weight of each pumpkin. She waved when she saw me.

"How's the competition looking?" I asked.

"Fierce," she answered, then made a face. "Grandma liked your dad's ideas, so now I'm grounded for a month too."

"Misery loves company," Dad said, coming up behind her. He handed me and Austin some change. "Why don't you two see if you can't find us all some coffee and donuts while we wait?"

Austin and I left the staging area. It was still early, and all over the farm volunteers were running around getting things ready before the festival officially started. I heard a few whispers as we walked, and I was pretty sure I heard someone say, "Right there, Stan. That's *her.* That's the Star Bandit."

I think Austin heard too, because he said, "You could have told me you were the Star Bandit, you know."

I shrugged. "I guess."

We walked side by side, neither of us saying anything. Our arms accidentally bumped each other, and we both split apart fast, like our skin had been seared. I wished we could go back to last summer, when all either of us cared about was who made the most free throws. If I liked

Austin and Violet was right and Austin liked me . . . then what was supposed to happen next?

Over by the Caulfields' red barn, food stands had been set up, and Don, from Don's Donuts, waved and called us over. "Izzy Malone! I owe you one huge thank-you! My star donuts are selling like hotcakes. Business has never been so great!"

"How much are they?" I asked. "My dad and Mr. Jackson want some coffee and donuts."

"For the Star Bandit, they're on the house! I'm competing in the regatta too. I was just about to let my wife take over." He gestured to a slight woman in overalls. "I've got my pumpkin over at the staging area, waiting to be weighed. Named him the Death Star. You want me to bring them the coffee and donuts?"

"Sure," I said. "I need to go help out at my mom's booth anyways, so that would be great."

After Don left I turned to Austin. "So . . . I guess I'll see you later?"

"Sure." He plunged his hands into his pockets and took a deep breath. "I was thinking . . . Do you want to eat lunch with me sometime?"

He was pink-cheeked, and I think we both knew he was asking more than if I just wanted to eat lunch with him. But if I said yes, did that mean we'd have to become one of those lame couples at school who stared into each other's eyes and generally looked like they'd lost a piece of their brain?

"I mean," Austin rushed on, when I didn't answer, "we could get lunch today. Like a hamburger, maybe."

The word "hamburger" made me think of something. "Do you have a cell phone?" I asked.

"Uh, yeah," he said, sounding confused. "Why?"

"'Cause I need to borrow it."

Austin still looked confused, but he dug into his pocket and pulled out his phone.

Sophia picked up on the second ring. "Hey, Sophia? It's Izzy. Are you going to Pumpkin Palooza today? . . . Do you think you could bring me something?" Quickly, I told her what I needed.

"What was that all about?" Austin asked when I handed back his phone.

"Nothing." I paused. "Look—I'm going to pass on lunch."

"You mean lunch today?"

"No. I mean, lunch *any* day."

"Oh. Right, cool. I get it."

From the look on Austin's face, it was clear he *did* get

it. We may not have been able to go back to the way things were, but that didn't mean I wanted to move forward, either. On Thursday when Daisy, Violet, Sophia, and I ate lunch together, Sophia said maybe we should start eating together every day, and we all said yes. I wasn't about to mess that up for a boy, no matter how good he was at basketball.

"I just don't think I'm ready for lunch," I said.

"Well, then . . . maybe we could still shoot hoops every now and then?" Austin asked hopefully.

"Sure," I said. "As long as you don't mind losing to my superior skills," I added.

"Superior, nothing. The next time we play, prepare to be crushed." Austin grinned and turned to head back to the staging area. "Good luck at the regatta!"

Maybe one day I'd be ready for lunch, and holding hands, and all that weird stuff. But for today, I was happy to shoot free throws with my friend.

32

SLEDGEHAMMERS
AND OPEN DOORS

The festival was starting to get busier as I made my way to Mom's campaign booth. Near the Caulfields' farmhouse, bored-looking teenagers were manning the game stations while kids tossed footballs through tire swings or pennies onto glass plates. A bunch of boys dressed in their Halloween costumes were running around playing tag in the Caulfields' pumpkin patch.

Over at Mom's booth, Aunt Mildred and Grandma Bertie were busy passing out star donuts and MALONE FOR MAYOR stickers.

"*I said*, only take one," Aunt Mildred snapped at a

lanky teenage boy who was trying to shove a handful of donuts into his backpack.

"Where have you been?" Mom demanded. "You should have been here an hour ago."

"I went to get Dad coffee," I answered, but she wasn't really listening.

"Look over there," she said. Across the way, Mayor Franklin's booth was giving away free sodas and candy. "Of all the places Kendra could set up her booth, she had to choose directly across from me. It's insulting."

"It's politics," Grandma Bertie said cheerfully. "And take it as a compliment, dear. It means she's starting to see you as competition."

"It's about time," Mom grumbled. "The election is in a week and a half." She frowned. "We should have given out soda and candy too."

"Janine, no one is going to vote for Kendra just because she gave out better snacks," Aunt Mildred said.

"Milly's right," Grandma Bertie agreed. "I personally always vote for the candidate with the best hair, and Kendra Franklin could really use some help in that department, so I don't think you have anything to worry about."

Aunt Mildred looked thoroughly disgusted, but she

kept quiet. The sun came out, and the day started warming up. The booth had a steady stream of visitors, and for a while Aunt Mildred, Grandma Bertie, and I were busy passing out stickers and donuts while Mom answered questions about her campaign. A couple people marched up to tell her exactly what they thought about me being the Star Bandit. But each time, Aunt Mildred accidentally spilled her coffee on them, so they didn't get too far with their complaining.

Sophia came by with her family. Her mom reached over and pulled me into a hug. "Thank you," she whispered in my ear.

"For what?" I asked, surprised.

"Sophia is much happier about living in Dandelion Hollow since you two became friends. She had a great time making cupcakes with you girls."

"Oh, no problem," I said. I was just glad Mrs. Ramos didn't seem to be mad.

Over at the other end of the booth, Sophia was introducing her brothers, David and Diego, to Aunt Mildred and Grandma Bertie. "See," she said, "Izzy has twins in her family too."

"Wow," said David (or maybe it was Diego). "You're *really* old!"

Grandma Bertie threw back her head and laughed, but Aunt Mildred just scowled. Mrs. Ramos and her brothers moved on to the next booth. I pulled Sophia aside and whispered, "Do you have it?"

"Yes." Sophia produced a tiny silver box. "I hope she likes it."

"Me too." I shoved the box into my pocket before anyone noticed it, and Sophia left to catch up with her family, saying she'd meet me at the pond before the regatta started later that afternoon.

Things picked up, and Mom was constantly shaking hands or answering questions, although the line over at Mayor Franklin's booth was always much longer. Violet and her dad came by. They were with Ms. Harmer; her daughter, Olivia; and a little boy who looked about the same age as Sophia's brothers.

"Dad and Ms. Harmer wanted our families to spend time together," Violet said as they passed by. "After the regatta, we're all going out to eat. And I am grounded for a month because of all the Star Bandit stuff. It would have been only two weeks, but Ms. Harmer said it should be four, just like you. Do you believe that?" she whispered furiously. "He let her help decide my punishment."

Violet and her family moved on, and when things

slowed down Grandma Bertie and Aunt Mildred left to take a break. Once Mom and I were alone, she said, "The picture was a mistake."

"What?" I turned toward her, but Mom wasn't looking at me. She kept her gaze forward, smiling at passersby.

"The fliers you saw on Ms. Zubov's porch, with the picture of me and Dad and Carolyn? It was a mistake. Carolyn needed to send in a couple pictures for a summer music camp she's trying to get into, so we took it while we were waiting for you to change your clothes. There must have been a mistake at the printer—the flier was always supposed to have been of the four of us." Mom turned and faced me. "Do you believe me, Isabella?"

"Izzy," I said before I could stop myself. Now that I thought about it, I *did* remember Carolyn saying something about music camp and needing photos. "I believe you," I said. "And I really didn't mean to damage your campaign stuff," I added. "I'm not gonna lie, I was flaming mad angry when I saw the mailer, but my temper stops short of intentional delinquency."

"That's a relief," Mom said, but she was smiling. Then she sighed. "I know what I said last night was out of line, and I'm sorry for that. . . . You know, your sister is the kind of person who doors will open for. She was

born naturally talented—it happens once in a million—
and I guess I get too caught up in it sometimes." She
glanced over at Mayor Franklin's booth, where there
was still a line waiting. "I'm not a one-in-a-million kind
of person—at least, not in that way. I always wanted to
be, but I'm not. Doors don't open by themselves for me.
And sometimes, when doors won't open *for* you, you
have to try opening them yourself—even if that means
taking a sledgehammer to them. I guess that's what I'm
trying to do with this election. I know I probably won't
win, but I think I have some ideas that would really help
this town, and I'm giving it my best shot."

I thought about how I'd seen Mom talk to herself in
the mirror and how she kept trying to convince people to
support her for mayor—even when most everyone figured
she didn't stand a chance. I thought maybe we weren't so
different, after all.

"I can understand that," I said. "That's what I'm trying
to do with the regatta—I just want to open some doors."

"And if I know you," Mom said, "you're not afraid to
pick up that sledgehammer."

We smiled at each other, and in that moment it felt like
time inched forward a bit to the day when we would wake
up and no longer be strangers.

Mom glanced over by the pond. "You've been really helpful today—if you want to join your father, you're welcome to leave here a little early."

"No, I'm good," I said, picking up a few more MALONE FOR MAYOR stickers. "We've still got work to do."

And, I thought, checking to make sure I still had the box from Sophia tucked into my pocket, I had a little unfinished business to attend to.

33

HAMBURGERS AND
HOT DATES

I went to change into my gear for the regatta: a tank top, cutoffs, and flip-flops. When I returned to the booth, Grandma Bertie and Aunt Mildred were just coming back from their break, bringing with them a few teenage boys who were dragging wagons filled with crates of water bottles and boxes of granola bars. We'd run out of donuts by then, so they'd figured they should stock up on more supplies.

"It's much healthier than soda and candy and—Look!" Grandma Bertie cried. "Scooter McGee is on his way, and he's got flowers!"

"I don't need to look," Aunt Mildred said, opening up

a box of granola bars. "I'm not going to lunch with him. I changed my mind."

"Changed your mind?" Grandma Bertie repeated. "You can't change your mind. You already said yes."

"I can do whatever I darn well please, Bertha. Just because you're six minutes older than me doesn't mean—"

"Hello, Mildred!" Scooter said, holding out a bundle of orange tulips. "Are you ready for our hot date?"

"Actually—"

"Aunt Mildred, can I talk to you for a sec?" I pulled her toward the back of the booth and showed her the tiny silver box Sophia gave me. "This is for you. It's a present. It's from—"

"I know where it's from, Isabella—I'm not an imbecile." With a grunt, Aunt Mildred took the box and lifted the lid. Inside was the hamburger charm I'd seen at Charming Trinkets. "What's this for?" she asked.

"I bought this for you for your date today," I said. She started to argue, but I rushed on, "Your story isn't done yet, Aunt Mildred. You still have memories you can make. Go have lunch with Scooter. Go out there and earn your charm."

"Yes, Mildred, throw the poor man a bone," Grandma Bertie said, coming up behind us. "He's liked you ever since we were sophomores in high school." Her voice softened. "Jack would have wanted you to go, Milly. You know he would've."

The lines on Aunt Mildred's face seemed to fall away, and all of a sudden she looked younger and . . . softer, somehow. "Yes, I suppose he would have," she said.

"Great." I took back the silver box. "You can have this once you've earned it."

"Well, you don't have to be so bossy about it." She squared her shoulders and yelled, "Scooter! I'm thoroughly hungry—I require a hamburger!"

"Your wish is my command," Scooter replied, offering her his arm.

"That was very nice of you, dear," Grandma Bertie said as we watched them walk away. "That hamburger is decades overdue."

34

THE GREAT PUMPKIN REGATTA

A giant pumpkin decorated like a pirate ship and sporting a skull-and-crossbones flag was being lifted by a crane as I walked up to Caulfield Pond. Spectators were taking their places around the edges of the shore, and Scooter was fiddling with the microphone. "Turn it up!" he hollered to Mr. Barnaby, who was working the sound system.

The crane settled the pirate pumpkin into the water, next to four other pumpkin boats. One of them—Don's Death Star—was covered in *Star Wars* stickers and was much smaller than the others. "I told you it was too small! How am I supposed to sit in that?" he complained to his wife.

Mike Harrison stood on Don's other side, armed with his paddle, as the crane, making a warning *beep-beep* sound, started lifting his pumpkin. On his head, Mr. Harrison wore a crown shaped like a pumpkin. "Three-peat, three-peat, three-peat," chanted his family. All of them were wearing pumpkin crowns too.

"I hope Harrison's pumpkin sinks," Dave Miller, owner of Miller's General Store and of the pirate ship pumpkin, grumbled to his wife. He was dressed as a pirate, complete with an eye patch and a stuffed parrot on his shoulder.

"I'm sure you'll win this year," his wife answered.

Dad and Mr. Jackson were to the right of Mr. Harrison, and they had done a great job hollowing out Bozo and turning him into a boat. A number four was stuck to Bozo's back, and Dad waved when he saw me. "We're all ready for you," he called.

My flip-flops sank into the mud and icy water closed over my toes as I stepped into the pond. I sucked in a breath and waded out to Dad and Mr. Jackson.

I started to climb into Bozo, but Violet's voice rang out, "Izzy, wait!"

Violet, Daisy, and Sophia came wading out into the pond. Sophia was carrying a large plastic bag.

"We are your designated pit crew," Daisy said. "Sophia had a great idea for team T-shirts. Show her."

Sophia flashed a bashful smile. "It was nothing, really. I just figured by now most people would know you're the Star Bandit, and if they didn't, well, what better way to tell them than at the race?" She pulled an orange T-shirt from the bag. It had the words TEAM STAR BANDIT in black block letters across the front and back.

"We also figured Bozo could use some decorative flourishes." Violet held up a pack of glittery star stickers. "What do you say?"

I laughed. "Sounds good to me."

I pulled a T-shirt on over my tank top while Violet, Daisy, and Sophia started decorating Bozo. After they were finished, Dad and Mr. Jackson held Bozo steady while I clambered in. The fit was a little tight, and the inside of the pumpkin felt cold and slimy, and I was pretty sure my legs would be asleep by the time the race was over.

"Can I have your attention, ladies and gentlemen?" Scooter said into the microphone. "The regatta will begin in two minutes! Racers, make your final adjustments!"

"Ready?" Dad asked, handing me my paddle.

"Ready," I said.

"Okay—go out there and give it all you've got! Girls—would you like to push Izzy to the starting line?"

Dad and Mr. Jackson changed places with Daisy, Violet, and Sophia, and they pushed me up to the red ribbon stretched between two trees over the pond.

"What's *she* doing here?" Daisy asked suddenly.

Decked out in her own pumpkin boat and wearing one of her mother's campaign shirts was Stella. A couple of the Paddlers, including Lauren, pushed Stella into position, right next to me.

"Good luck," Lauren said, with a meaningful glance at me. "May the best woman win," she added.

"At this time," Scooter called, "I'd like to ask all crew assistants to leave the pond."

"We'll be cheering for you!" Sophia said, and Daisy and Violet waved as they all waded back to shore.

"What are you doing here?" I whispered to Stella.

"The same thing you're doing here," she said. "Trying to win this stupid race."

"It's not stupid."

"Sure it is," Stella said, sounding furious. "But try telling that to my mom and Lauren."

She turned away, and I looked out at the spectators. Aunt Mildred was standing next to Scooter—I couldn't tell for sure, but it looked like she was actually laughing at something he was saying. Grandma Bertie was standing next to Ms. Zubov; they both waved when they saw me looking at them. Dad, Mr. Jackson, and Austin were on the other side of the pond. As I watched, Carolyn came running up to them, her guitar case strapped around her chest. The only person I didn't see from my family was Mom.

The Paddlers were standing next to Mayor Franklin, and Lauren nodded at me when our eyes locked. *This is it*, I told myself. *Win this, and you can be one of them. Quick, elegant strokes.* I closed my eyes and visualized myself sailing past the finish line.

"Ladies and gentlemen!" Scooter's voice boomed out across the pond. "Welcome to Dandelion Hollow's annual Great Pumpkin Regatta! We have a slew of worthy competitors, so today's race promises to be a gourd show! Get it? Gourd show?" The audience groaned, and he continued, "Pumpkin number one, hailing from the distinguished Harrison family—our two-time defending champions—and weighing in at eight hundred and fifty-three pounds . . . I give you . . . the Pumpkin King!"

There was scattered applause, and more than a few boos, while the Harrison family chanted, "Three-peat, three-peat," again, in case nobody heard them the first time.

"In pumpkin number two, representing Miller's General Store, we have Dave Miller himself, weighing in at eight hundred and two pounds! Not Dave, but his pumpkin, Captain Jack O. Lantern!"

Tons of applause, and Scooter continued, "And pumpkin number three . . ." He paused while Aunt Mildred whispered in his ear. "I apologize, pumpkin number three, the Death Star, has been disqualified due to insufficient size. Better luck next year, Don—perhaps you should stop eating so many of your donuts!

"Pumpkin number four, and my personal favorite, weighing in at five hundred and fifty-two pounds, we have Bozo, which will be captained by none other than Izzy Malone, Dandelion Hollow's own Star Bandit!"

Mixed applause, and a couple people booed until Ms. Zubov yelled, "My garden's never looked so good! Thanks, Izzy!"

While Scooter announced a few more racers, I kept my eyes glued to the buoy across the way and kept imagining myself zooming across the pond, and being first to cross the finish line.

"And last but not least! We have a last-minute surprise entry. Stella Franklin, daughter of our illustrious and long, long, *long*-serving Mayor Franklin. Weighing in at five hundred and sixty pounds, I give you . . . the Pumpkin Paddler!"

Of course, there was a ton of applause for Stella.

"All right, ladies and gentlemen, the rules are simple: Each racer must paddle their pumpkin around the buoy in the center of the pond and then head back this way. The first to cross the finish line wins. Ready?"

"Ready!" the crowd yelled.

"Good! On your mark . . . get set . . . go!"

And we were off! I dug my paddle into the water and rowed as fast as I could. Working out on Dad's rowing machine had given me good strength, but, just like Dad had said, it was definitely more awkward racing a giant pumpkin instead of a thin kayak.

Mike Harrison and Dave Miller shot in front of the rest of us, and my heart sank a bit, but I wasn't going down without a fight. Both of them had big, heavy guts, and I was willing to bet this race was the one time they worked out all year.

I dipped my oar into the water and imagined I was back in my garage on Dad's rowing machine: *One, two; one, two.*

"Pumpkin number five, Mr. Pumpkin Head, is taking on water," Scooter called. "Ladies and gentlemen, it looks like we've got a sinker!"

Mr. Pumpkin Head's racer wasn't giving up, though. He ditched his oars and started trying to swim the pumpkin out to the buoy. It was a lost cause, though, and soon Mr. Pumpkin Head was sinking fast.

"And it's going . . . going . . . gone!" Scooter yelled. "Just like the *Titanic*, folks, pumpkin number five is out of commission! But I suppose our hearts must go on!"

Stella and I were both slowly gaining on Mike Harrison and Dave Miller. They reached the buoy first and their pumpkins collided as they came around the bend, spinning them both off course. "You did that on purpose!" Mike shouted.

"Did not!" Dave shouted back. He ripped off his eye patch. "Can't see anything with this thing on!"

Stella and I gave them a wide berth as we paddled around the buoy and shot out in front of them.

"And it's the Star Bandit vs. the Pumpkin Paddler," Scooter called. "Who will win folks? It's Izzy—no, it's Stella. . . . They're in a dead heat, my friends! Hang on to your pumpkins, 'cause this one's gonna be close!"

I glanced over. Stella was right next to me, her tongue poking out the side of her mouth as she furiously paddled. I dug and dug. My strokes weren't elegant, but fast and frantic, until Stella's paddle clipped mine. Bozo spun and crashed into her pumpkin, and our paddles crossed.

"Stop it!" Stella yelled as we tried to untangle our paddles.

"I didn't do anything!" I yelled back. "And why do you even care? You said this race is stupid!"

"It *is* stupid! But Lauren's made it clear I'd better beat you—and my mom told me I'd embarrass her if I lost to a weirdo like you."

Stella splashed water in my eyes. I sat back—stunned both by the water and her words—and Stella, finally untangling her paddle, edged past me. For the first time I wondered if living with Mayor Franklin might be a whole lot worse than living with Mom, and I actually felt bad for Stella.

Not enough to let her win, though.

I righted my boat, dug my paddle into the water, and continued on.

"The Pumpkin Paddler is in the lead!" Scooter yelled. "It looks like Stella Franklin is about to . . . But wait! It looks like Bozo is gaining. Yes, yes . . . Bozo and the Pumpkin Paddler are neck and neck, or perhaps I should say gourd and gourd! Here it comes, ladies and gentlemen: the final push! The big finale, the one squash to rule them all. . . . Yes, yes . . . *Yes!* It looks like it's Bozo! Pumpkin number four, helmed by our very own Izzy Malone, Dandelion Hollow's infamous Star Bandit, has just won! Izzy Malone is the newest winner of the Great Pumpkin Regatta!"

The crowd erupted into cheers. Violet, Daisy, and Sophia splashed into the pond and hugged me. Dad and Mr. Jackson also waded in, to help me climb out of Bozo. Once I was back on shore, a crowd surrounded me. A golden pumpkin trophy was thrust into my hands, and Scooter handed me a check for five hundred dollars, while Aunt Mildred, Grandma Bertie, and Carolyn came over to congratulate me.

"You were amazing!" Carolyn said, high-fiving me while Grandma Bertie took a picture of us.

"Thanks," I said, and looked around. "Where's Mom?"

"I'm right here!"

Mom came bursting through the crowd. She threw her arms around me. "I'm so proud of you!" When she pulled away, she pointed to a man holding a camera.

"This is Timothy Dalton, from the *Dandelion Gazette*. I thought we could take another shot at our campaign family photo."

"Now?" I looked down at myself. I was damp from the

waist down, and my cutoffs were smeared with orange pumpkin guts.

"Yes, now." Mom gave me a searching look. "Is that okay, Izzy?"

"Okay," I said, and I realized that might have been the first time she'd called me Izzy, without being reminded to.

"Everyone gather around Izzy," Dad said.

"Oh, dear," Grandma Bertie said, running her hands through her hair. "How do I look?"

"Fabulous," Aunt Mildred said. "You look just like me, don't you?"

"I look better than you, dear. I always have."

"Ew, Izzy," Carolyn said, wrinkling her nose. "You smell like a pumpkin autopsy."

"You know you love it," I said, slinging an arm around her as we all posed and waited for Mr. Dalton, who seemed to be having trouble with his camera.

"Mildred, you're pushing me," Grandma Bertie said.

"I'm not pushing you. Carolyn's pushing *me*."

"That's because Izzy's stepping on my foot," Carolyn said.

"Sorry," I said, stepping away.

"Bertha!" Aunt Mildred snapped. "Now *you're* pushing *me*."

"That's not pushing. *This* is pushing!"

"Stop it!" Aunt Mildred hollered.

"Watch it!" Carolyn yelled.

"Say cheese!" Mr. Dalton said.

When I looked at the photo later, Aunt Mildred and Grandma Bertie were smacking each other with their handbags, Mom and Carolyn were grabbing for Carolyn's guitar case before it fell into the pond, and Dad's face was frozen in a pained grimace. I was in the middle of it all, holding up my pumpkin trophy, and wearing my Team Star Bandit shirt.

It probably wasn't the shot of the picture-perfect family Mom was hoping for. But it was pretty much what we all really looked like: messy and out of place, and a million light-years away from normal.

35

PADDLING ALONE
(BUT NOT REALLY)

Eventually, the crowd started drifting away from the pond and back toward the games and food. Abandoned pumpkin boats bobbed in the water. Dad and Mr. Jackson were chatting with Scooter and Aunt Mildred while I pushed Bozo up to the edge of the shore.

Lauren appeared in front of me, the water lapping at the edges of her sandals. "Okay," she said.

"Okay, what?" I said, as I started peeling stickers off Bozo.

"The Paddlers. You're in, Stella's out."

I looked up. "Just like that?" The rest of the Paddlers

stood behind Lauren, all except for Stella, who still sat in her pumpkin boat, staring glumly off into the distance. "Isn't there room on the team for both of us?"

"Stella isn't cutting it," Lauren said. "So she's out. You're in."

"Thanks," I said, although the rush of excitement I expected to feel didn't come.

Ever since last summer, all I wanted was to join the Paddlers. I felt like it would mean that someone cared, that I wasn't as alone as I thought. That someone noticed. Because, up until recently, it seemed like no one had.

But somehow in the last month, almost without me realizing it, things had changed.

Behind the Paddlers, Aunt Mildred had approached, and was quietly listening.

"Practice is Saturdays at nine a.m. at the aquatic center," Lauren said. "Don't be late."

I imagined spending Saturday after Saturday with Lauren and . . . actually, I couldn't even name the other girls on the team. They all looked so much alike, I could never tell them apart.

"Thanks," I said again. "But . . . I think I'm going to pass." I couldn't believe the words were coming out of my mouth, but I knew I was making the right decision.

Don't get me wrong. I still loved racing, and the beauty of the open water, and the peace of a clear blue sky. But being on Lauren's team seemed a lot less appealing than it had a few months ago. Even if I wasn't a part of the Paddlers, that didn't mean I couldn't try out for the team at Dandelion High in a few years. And I would.

Aunt Mildred was smiling, but Lauren looked shocked. "What are you talking about? We both know you were desperate to join us."

"You're right," I said. "But I'm saying no anyway. For now I think I'd prefer to paddle alone."

Except I knew I wouldn't be alone. I had Daisy, Violet, and Sophia, and being friends with them beat being a part of the Paddlers any day.

Lauren—who was normally so cool—was looking more and more like a toddler about to throw a temper tantrum. I wondered how often she heard the word "no."

"Fine," she snapped. "Just so you know, everyone was sick of you following us around like a sad puppy—I only offered out of charity."

Charity? After I just won the race? I'd like to give *her* a little charity of my own.

My temper was rising, and my fingers and toes were

itching with options: launch pumpkin guts at her nasty-swinging ponytail, kick mud and water at her face . . . The possibilities were endless.

I think Aunt Mildred knew what I was thinking, because she shook her head and mouthed, *Butterfly.*

Reluctantly, I nodded, and decided I'd have to settle for a response of the purely verbal variety. I thought real hard about my next words: "Thank you. Your charitable efforts are noted and appreciated. But I'm still going to have to decline. I'll be sure to let everyone know you invited me to join, though!"

Lauren spun on her heel so fast the Paddlers had to scatter to get out of her way. They re-formed themselves and left, their ponytails swinging in unison.

"Congratulations," Aunt Mildred said as we watched them leave. "I think you just graduated from charm school." She held out a tiny silver box. "And to celebrate, it's *my* turn to give *you* a present."

I took the box and opened it. Inside was the glittery orange pumpkin charm I'd seen at Charming Trinkets.

"Add it to your bracelet later," Aunt Mildred said. "It's part of your story now."

The pumpkin charm sparkled in the afternoon sun, and I wondered if it was the last one she'd ever give me, now that I'd just graduated. It seemed to me that as soon as Mrs. Whippie—Aunt Mildred—had started sending me letters and charms, life had gotten crazy and strange, in the best possible way.

All of a sudden, I knew exactly how I wanted to spend my Saturdays. I looked up and said, "Hey, Aunt Mildred . . . What are you doing next weekend?"

THE BEGINNING
OF A GOOD STORY

"What if we called it 'The Charm Girls Club'?" I asked Aunt Mildred. It was the Saturday after Pumpkin Palooza, and we were walking to the Kaleidoscope Café, on our way to meet Daisy, Violet, and Sophia. The three of them had been excited to learn that Aunt Mildred was actually Mrs. Whippie, especially after she had convinced everyone's parents to give us a two-hour reprieve from our grounding.

"The Charm Girls Club," Aunt Mildred repeated, testing it out. "I like it."

"I thought we could meet every couple weeks or so."

Aunt Mildred nodded. "You'll just have to make sure it doesn't get in the way of your cleanup duties."

On Monday, I'd gone into Principal Chilton's office and given him my entire winnings from the regatta—five hundred dollars—to pay back the cleanup costs for the orange wall. Any money left over, I'd said, could be donated to the Eco Club, so they could still go on their trip to the observatory.

Overall, he took the news that I was the Star Bandit pretty well. After I was finished apologizing profusely and promising him that something like this would never, ever, *ever* happen again, he leaned forward and whispered, "I actually liked your orange wall. But there's no money in the school budget to repaint, and I doubt I could get our board of supervisors to agree to it even if there was, so unfortunately the gray walls will have to stay."

Then he straightened up and said he was giving me, Daisy, and Violet two weeks of detention. He also assigned us to Dandelion Middle's newly formed Cleanup Committee—which was just a fancy way of saying he wanted us on trash pickup duty for a couple months. Sophia said she didn't want to be left out, so she joined the committee too. I think she was the only one who was actually excited about it.

When Aunt Mildred and I arrived at the Kaleidoscope, Daisy, Violet, and Sophia were already there. They were huddling in a corner booth. Daisy and Sophia each had an arm around Violet, who was crying.

"What's wrong?" Aunt Mildred asked as we slid in across from them.

Violet wiped her face with the back of her hand. "Dad sat me down and talked to me today. He and Ms. Harmer are engaged."

"That stinks," I said, and Aunt Mildred rammed me with her elbow.

"Ow! I mean, that's . . . not totally terrible," I said, and scooted away from Aunt Mildred.

"That's not all," Violet said, beginning to sob again. "They don't want a long engagement, so they're getting married next week. They're already in contract to buy a new house—so we can all move in together and be one big happy family." Violet hung her head. "Dad said he hoped I'd try to be happy for him."

"Oh Violet, I'm so sorry." I couldn't imagine having the Hammer for a stepmother—I couldn't imagine having any mother besides my own. She had her problems, and most of the time neither of us understood each other, but I wouldn't have traded her for anyone. It made me mad that Violet had lost hers so young.

Aunt Mildred produced some scented tissues from

her handbag for Violet to dry her eyes. Ms. Zubov arrived
with plates of pumpkin pie. "Best of the season," she said,
passing them around. "They're on the house." She reached
over to squeeze Violet's hand. "I heard about your Dad's
engagement—"

"That's because this town is full of gossiping busy-
bodies," Aunt Mildred said.

"—and you can come here as often as you want, on the
house," Ms. Zubov finished.

Violet nodded, and we began eating our pie in silence.

"What's going on?" Violet asked after she'd stopped
crying. "Why did you want to meet today?"

"I had a lot of fun earning my charms," I began. "And
I thought . . . maybe you did too?" I waited, and the other
girls nodded. "So how would you feel about starting a
club? Maybe we could call ourselves the Charm Girls.
Aunt Mildred has agreed to keep buying us charms and
giving us tasks to do."

When I had told Aunt Mildred my idea and asked if she
wanted to be our official club leader, she teared up a little.

"I had a wonderful time picking out charms for you
girls, and I'd love to keep doing it," Aunt Mildred said
now. "In fact . . ." With great ceremony, she removed four
small boxes wrapped in pearl-pink wrapping paper, and

topped with white bows. "I've got another charm for you to earn, if you're up for the task."

The girls looked thoroughly intrigued. "You mean," Sophia said slowly, "we'd get together, do fun things, and add charms to our bracelets?"

"Something like that," Aunt Mildred said. "Speaking of which"—she produced a bracelet and a cupcake charm, which she handed to Sophia—"these are for you."

Sophia grinned widely as she hooked the charm onto her bracelet, and Violet said, "Yes, please. Can we be a club? The last thing I want to do is hang out with Melanie all the time—that's what I'm supposed to call Ms. Harmer at home." Her voice broke on the word "home," and she grabbed tightly onto Daisy and Sophia like she was afraid they'd vanish.

"I'm in," Sophia said, hugging Violet. "Earning my charm and baking those cupcakes was the most fun I've had since moving to Dandelion Hollow."

"I'm in, too," Daisy said.

"All right, then." Aunt Mildred passed the boxes around. "Go ahead and open them—I've talked to each of your parents, and they've already agreed to this. Izzy's parents have already said they'd be chaperones."

Exchanging curious glances, Violet, Daisy, and Sophia

each dug into their present, quickly ripping off the paper and bow. I went slower since I already knew what was inside.

"What's this for?" Daisy held up a tiny hot air balloon charm.

"I hope none of you are scared of heights," Aunt Mildred said. "Because next month—when you're all off grounding—you're going hot air ballooning!"

Sophia and Daisy cheered, and even Violet managed a smile, and when Ms. Zubov came back to our table, we all ordered second slices of pie to celebrate the beginning of our new club.

I was glad to have Violet back in my life, glad to be getting to know Daisy and Sophia, and I couldn't wait until next month, when we could all go hot air ballooning. I wanted to feel my feet rising, and look out and see the whole earth spread out before me. I wanted to fly so high my fingertips brushed the sky.

I wanted to soar.

But I didn't want to do it alone. I wanted Daisy, Violet, and Sophia right next to me.

If life is a story, I was figuring out who I wanted to star in mine.

ACKNOWLEDGMENTS

Once upon a time, several years ago in a cabin in Pollock Pines, I was enjoying a moment with my Journey Girls, my soul sisters, when my friend Cara Lane turned to me and said, "You should write a book about us." Now, writing a novel about six thirty-something women didn't particularly strike me as something I wanted to do, and I never base my characters on real people. But still, something about her comment stayed with me. In my more reflective moments, I like to imagine Izzy as a grown woman, with children of her own, telling them the story of how she met the best friends of her life. So thank you, Cara—a comment that you probably don't remember played a role in planting the seeds that one day grew into the pages of this book.

Thank you to my first reader, Ruth Gallo, who took the time on a park bench in Sonoma to read my first chapters, and told me to keep going.

To Noah Lundquist, my second reader, who, after finishing the first forty pages told me he wished I'd written more, because he wanted to finish it. Noah, the fact that you were so enthusiastic gave me the motivation to keep working, even on the days when the writing was hard, and I didn't think I'd ever be able to finish. Thank you, too, for helping me proofread my first pass pages, your feedback was incredibly helpful!

To Thomas Lundquist, who first clued me in to the existence of Star-Spangled Sunsets, I love the way you look at the world.

To Milo Smith, whose views on instructions versus imagination shaped my thinking as I developed Izzy's character.

To Deanna and Dave Bosley, Deana and Mark Lewis, Matt and Val Smith, Kelly and Ken Vogel, and Nancy and Gerry Winkler, as well as Pam and Tom Carroll and Lisa and Bryan Allen—all of you provided childcare when I desperately needed some quiet time to write, and I am grateful for each one of you.

To Alyson Heller, Ilaria Falorsi, Jessica Handelman, and everyone else at Simon & Schuster, thank you for taking such good care of my book baby!

To Kerry Sparks, thank you for being, as always, my Agent of Awesome.

To Mike Troyan, and all the staff at the Citrus Heights

Barnes & Noble, thank you for always taking such good care of me at my launch parties!

To the friends, bloggers, librarians, and reviewers who have supported me and my books over the years, I am so grateful for you all.

Thank you especially to Ryan Lundquist, my first and fiercest fan, I love you like crazy.

And finally to God and His Son, the author of my own story, who is deeply vested in all our stories, help me to see all of humanity through the loving lens of your own eyes.

Turn the page for a look at

THE WONDROUS WORLD OF
VIOLET BARNABY

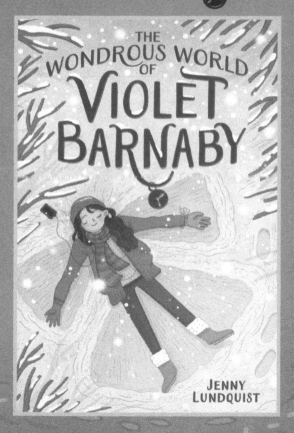

CHAPTER 1

SHABBY SWEAT-
SHIRTS

I have a glittery purple journal where I keep word lists. Each list has a different title, like Words I Love, Funny Words, or Words That Annoy Me. On my list of Words I Love, I have "sparkling," "bubbling," and "spinning" because they remind me of parties and people smiling and no tears at all. It's my favorite list. But it's been a long time since I added anything to it.

I also have a list of Words I Don't Like. Words like "bucolic," which means "relating to rural life," but reminds me of the flu, and makes me queasy every time I hear it. Then there are words I despise, words that can wrap around your heart and squeeze you until you feel like you can't breathe anymore.

For my dad and me, that word is "cancer."

"Cancer"—It's on the top of my Words I Hate list. But last month, I added a new word just below it:

"Stepmother."

For Halloween most kids got a bucketful of candy. I got a stepmother. And not just any stepmother, either. Nope. My dad couldn't meet a nice lady over the Internet like a normal person. No, he had to go and marry Ms. Melanie Harmer—aka the Hammer—the meanest teacher at Dandelion Middle School.

Dad and Melanie got engaged at the end of October, but they didn't want the hassle of a long engagement. So while other kids were putting away their Halloween costumes and trading candy with their friends, I was putting on my old Easter dress and trying not to puke the whole way over to the county courthouse, where it took the judge less than ten minutes to pronounce Dad and Melanie man and wife.

As I stood there, watching them kiss, I wondered what it would be like to live with the Hammer and her two kids—Olivia, who's my age; and Joey, who's eight—in the house Dad and Melanie bought.

Now, nearly a month later, it was the Saturday after Thanksgiving. Moving Day. Dad and I were in Dad's soon-to-be-vacated bedroom. The moving people had taken almost everything out of the house. We had just a few things to pack up before we left the only house I'd ever lived in forever. With all the furniture gone, it didn't seem like a real home anymore. Of course, it hadn't felt like a real home for the last year and a half, since Mom died.

I swept the floor while Dad went through a box of old clothes. Once I finished with the broom I checked "Sweep Dad's Floor" off the cleaning list I'd made. The list was two pages long, but I was almost finished with it. Dad wanted the house to be spotless before he gave the keys to his real estate agent.

Dad held up a green T-shirt. "What do you think? Keep or toss?"

"Toss, definitely," I said. "It has holes in the sleeves."

Dad stared at it and frowned. "I guess. But I could find a use for it. Maybe when I paint?"

"Dad, we talked about this," I reminded him. "Toss it."

"Okay, okay." Dad moved it into the trash pile, and then pulled out a raggedy sweatshirt. "What about this one?"

"Mom gave you that one, remember?" I said.

Dad flushed, and hurriedly put it into his "for keeps" pile, muttering that he was sorry, and I felt like a big jerk. The sweatshirt was really shabby and falling apart, and it's not like I thought that by throwing it out he was forgetting Mom. But sometimes I feel like he's packed up and moved into Melanie's life and left me behind. Like *I'm* an old sweatshirt that suddenly seems too small and too shabby. Maybe one day Dad had woken up and decided he'd outgrown his old life. Our life. Then he met Melanie.

While Dad finished going through the box, I consulted my list. Next up was "Vacuum Your Room," so I headed for my bedroom. I paused in the empty living room. Memories of my mom filled these rooms and they spun around me like dust motes dancing in the sunlight. I wondered if the new owners would know how happy our family had been here—before Mom got sick, that is. Would they know she used to sit by the fireplace and knit, or that there used to be a piano under the window where her music students would play during their afternoon lessons, or that next to that piano was a vintage record player where we played old records from her collection—always records, never a CD or an iPod, because she felt a true fan of music should have a decent record collection?

But now that piano was at my friend Izzy's house so

her sister Carolyn could use it, and our record collection, along with the rest of our furniture, was packed up and on its way to the new house—or on its way to the Goodwill, because Melanie said we no longer needed it.

My room didn't look like a real bedroom anymore, either. I stared at the purple walls as I ran the vacuum cleaner. Mom and I had painted them together; she'd even let me stay home from school one day to do it. A couple days later, after the paint had dried, she sat me down on my bed, and said, "I have something to tell you."

It's amazing how quickly six little words can change your entire life.

Next on my list was: "Wipe Down Dad's Closet."

I pulled a paint-splattered folding chair up to the top shelf and was about to get started when I saw a dusty red envelope pushed against the corner. I flipped it over. On the outside it read, "For Violet, For Christmas." I recognized the handwriting immediately.

It was my mother's.

CHAPTER 2

MEMORIES THAT WON'T GET MADE

"Dad! Dad, come in here!"

I must have sounded pretty panicky, because Dad came rushing in. His cell phone was ringing. By the ringtone—a shrill-sounding trumpet—I knew it was Melanie calling again. Apparently, the movers Dad had hired were completely incompetent, and for some reason she needed to call him every ten minutes to tell him so.

"What?" he said as he sent the call to voice mail. "What is it?" His face turned white when he saw the envelope. "Where did you get that?"

"I found it in your closet."

We stared at the letter, and Mom's swooping cursive,

until Dad sank onto the folding chair, and put his head in his hands. "I'm so sorry," he said, his voice sounding muffled. "I forgot—" His phone trumpeted. With an irritated grunt, he sent the call to voice mail again. "I completely forgot about that letter. I was supposed to have given it to you *last* December, but . . ."

He trailed off, but I understood. Last Christmas—Black Christmas, I called it privately—was our first one without Mom, and Dad had forgotten a lot of things. To put up a tree. To buy presents. To buy groceries. Sometimes it seemed like he even forgot I was in the room.

"Do you remember all those letters Mom wrote you when you were having trouble with spelling?" he asked.

I nodded. Mom used to write me long letters, using all the words on my spelling list. It was the highlight of the week for me, getting her notes. Pretty soon, I became the best speller in my class.

"Well . . . before she died, she wrote you a letter. She thought the holiday season might be hard for you. You know how much she loved Christmas."

I nodded again, but I hoped he wouldn't go into a big pep talk about holiday cheer. I had no interest in Christmas, or the holiday season at all. It was fine with me if we just skipped straight ahead to New Year's.

"I'm so sorry," Dad said. "I really didn't mean—" His phone rang again and he muttered a nasty word under his breath.

"You'd probably better answer it," I said. "She'll just keep calling."

"I'll text her." While Dad tapped on his phone, I stared at the letter, my heart pounding.

When someone you love dies, no one ever tells you that you've lost more than just that person. You've lost a lifetime of memories that won't get made. You've lost a lifetime of getting to hear that person's voice. But here in this letter were Mom's words, and I was sure when I read them, I'd hear her voice. A voice I missed so much I oftentimes felt sick inside.

"Do you want to read it now?" Dad asked. "Before . . ."

Before we go to the new house is what he meant. Melanie's house, a place Mom would never be.

Dad's cell pinged with a text, and we both glanced at the message: I NEED YOU HERE TO DIRECT THE MOVERS. THEY'RE IDIOTS!

"It's okay," I said. "I can read it later."

I shoved the letter into my backpack. As much as I wanted to tear it right open, I wanted to do it on my own time. When Melanie wasn't interrupting every two seconds—like a shrill alarm clock you just couldn't shut off.

CHAPTER
3

A NEW START

As Dad started up the car, I looked at our house one last time. The front door was made of worn, splintered wood and was painted a bright shade of red that Mom always said reminded her of ripe strawberries. The door got smaller and smaller as we drove down the street, until we turned the corner and it slipped from view altogether.

Here's something else that's red and worn and splintered: a heart that's been broken in two.

We were only moving to the next neighborhood over, but it felt like a million miles away, and my stomach heaved when the new house came into view. It was a big two-story that was painted brown with bright white shutters and trim. It also had a huge wraparound porch and a big bay window. It was exactly the kind of house Mom said she wanted to live in one day.

"Ready, Champ?" Dad asked as he shut the car off. He started calling me Champ after I'd won the fourth-grade spelling bee, and the name stuck. He was smiling, and as much as I didn't like Ms. Harm—Melanie—I at least appreciated that. Smiling Dad was much better than Crying Dad. Of course, he only ever cried at night, when he thought I was sleeping.

"I'm ready," I lied. "Let's go."

As we strode up the walkway, I ran my fingers along the golden charm bracelet I always wear on my wrist, and I felt a little better. My friends Izzy, Sophia, and Daisy have the same bracelet, and I was going to see them tomorrow night at the Dandelion Hollow Christmas-Tree-Lighting.

I just had to get through the next day and a half first.

The front yard was covered in boxes, and Melanie was arguing with one of the movers—a short, round man whose eyebrows looked like thick black slugs.

"What's going on?" Dad asked.

"The movers are quitting," Melanie said, shooting the man a withering glare.

"We're not quitting," he said, going red in the face. "I

just refuse to have my men continually berated because you couldn't be bothered to label your boxes."

"The boxes *are* labeled!" Melanie shouted.

"Where?" He spread his hands wide. "Show me, and my men will get back to work. Otherwise, we're leaving. We're not waiting around while you open every single box!"

"They were labeled!" Melanie insisted. "I don't know what happened!" Her eyes found mine. "Do you know anything about this?" she demanded.

I wanted so badly to say something snarky back to her. But Mom always said, "If you can't say something nice, it's better to say nothing at all." Consequently, I've spent a lot of the last month keeping my mouth shut.

"No, I just got here," I said, in a polite voice. *Not nearly enough time to screw anything up for you*, I added silently in a decidedly not-polite voice. Melanie had been irritated with me all week. All month, actually, ever since Dad had let her into our house and the two of them had started deciding what to keep and what they should donate. I overheard her in the kitchen telling Dad she "didn't appreciate my attitude" when they'd taken Joey, Olivia, and me to the new house to pick out our new bedrooms. I'd wanted to go marching in there and ask why I should be excited about it; none of the rooms in the new house were as good as the one she was making me leave behind.

The movers started packing up, and Melanie went scurrying after them. Dad scratched his head. "That's strange. I know we labeled them. Well . . . I guess we'd better get them all off the yard."

Dad picked up a box and headed inside. I grabbed one and nearly toppled over—it must have weighed a ton. Olivia, who'd been sitting on a rocker on the front porch while all of this was happening, said, "Careful, that one's heavy."

"Thanks for the tip," I snapped, dropping the box.

"Excuse me?" A deliveryman carrying a stack of pizzas came striding up to us. "I've got a delivery for a Mrs. Barnaby—is that your mother?"

"No," Olivia said, just as I answered, "Yes."

We glanced at each other and blinked. I realized he was talking about Melanie, not Mom. It made me sick that I had the same last name as the Hammer now—but at least she hadn't changed it yet at Dandelion Middle.

"I mean, yes, that's my mother," Olivia said, just as I said, "No."

The deliveryman sighed like he didn't have time for our nonsense. "Are you two sisters?"

"No," Olivia answered.

"Definitely not," I said.

"My mom's in the garage with the movers, I think," Olivia added.

"Yeah, just listen for the sound of shrill arguing, and you'll find her," I said.

The deliveryman sighed again and started for the garage. Olivia shot me a murderous look. Forget being sisters—Olivia and I weren't even friends. I'd met her for the first time last summer, not too long after Dad and Melanie started dating. I think since we were both starting sixth grade at Dandelion Middle, Melanie thought we'd become BFFs or something.

"Want to eat lunch together in the cafeteria?" Olivia had asked me the night before school started. She sounded about as excited as someone getting their tooth pulled, and I was pretty sure Melanie had put her up to it.

"I'm busy," I'd answered.

"Busy doing what?"

"I don't know yet," I'd said. "I just know I'm busy."

After that, we pretty much went out of our way to ignore each other at school.

I picked up a couple small boxes, and Olivia, still lounging on the porch, said, "Those belong in the living room."

"Way to be helpful," I said, and headed for the house.

Inside it smelled like disinfectant, and furniture was haphazardly pushed up against the walls. Half-opened boxes littered the floor. In the middle of the living room was a huge box of Melanie's Christmas decorations. I wanted to stomp all over them until they broke into tiny bits—she'd decided that Mom and Dad's decorations were too old and worn, so she sent most of them off to the Goodwill.

From the front door I heard Melanie shriek, "Who tracked mud into the house?"

I looked down at my tennis shoes. Oops.

"Those are Violet's footprints," Olivia was saying to Melanie, who was now carrying the stack of pizzas, when I reached the entryway. "She moved some boxes into the house."

"Because you *told* me to," I said.

"Um, hello? I didn't think I'd have to tell you to wipe your feet first. What are you, five? Why don't you go and 'help' somewhere else?" she said, making air quotes around the word "help."

"Fine—I've got better things to do, anyway," I said, thinking of Mom's letter.

"Olivia, cool it," Melanie warned as Dad joined us. "The mud will come out." To me, she said, "How was your drive over?" Like we'd taken a trip across the country, instead of a short ride across Thistle Street. Dad put his hand on my back, and I knew I had to answer nicely.

"It was fine. I'm going to miss my old room, though."

Melanie flushed, and Dad squeezed my shoulder, like I'd said something wrong, instead of just answering truthfully. Melanie asked Olivia to put the pizzas in the kitchen; then she led Dad and me upstairs, making chirpy comments about the house, and when she reached my new room she threw open the door, and said, "Isn't it great?"

I just smiled and nodded. Because if I was honest, the room was terrible; it looked even worse than I remembered. My mattress lay on the floor. A pile of boxes was stacked in the center—making the room look smaller than it already was. The walls were white and dusty, and the window was grimy.

It just didn't seem like someplace I could ever call my own.

Dad was smiling and staring at me expectantly. I searched for something nice to say: "These walls would look great in purple." I could already imagine it, and I knew Izzy would help me paint. She doesn't like boring walls, either. Last month, she got into a ton of trouble for painting a wall at school orange. Well, *we* got into a ton of trouble, because I helped her do it.

"Purple?" Melanie blinked, and chewed on her cheek. Sometimes when she does that, she looks like she's swallowing her lips.

"Yeah, I think I'll paint them purple. Just like my old room."

"I wasn't aware we were painting the walls," Melanie said, glancing at Dad, who suddenly looked uncomfortable.

Dad shifted back and forth, and I could tell he wished I hadn't said anything. "We'll have to figure it out later, won't we, Champ?" His smile dimmed, and more than anything else, I didn't want him to stop smiling.

"Dad never said I could paint the walls," I said quickly. "It's just, I painted my other room, and I guess I just assumed . . ."

"Well," Melanie said with forced cheerfulness, "we're all making a new start, aren't we? We'll talk about paint later."

"Sure," I said.

But I knew I'd be stuck with white walls for a long time.